# BEGINNING OF AN END

The guy never saw what had come for him. A two-hand chop at either side of the neck sat the guy down and shuttered the eyes without so much as a gasp of understanding. Bolan hoisted the unconscious man to his shoulder and headed for the front door. Throwing the double bolts, he stepped into the little security room that marked the final obstacle.

The guard had both feet on the desk, a Schmeisser one lunge away. Both feet crashed to the floor as he tried for it—a mere heartbeat removed from instant fame and glory, but a heartbeat too late. The Beretta spat once from the doorway, chugging its silent skullbuster toward a bone-shattering denial of fame and glory. The guard fell back into the chair and stayed there, the broken head slumped limply over the backrest.

The Executioner rolled chair and all into the darkened interior, then got the hell out of there with his prisoner. As he rejoined the night, he knew that it had been a successful mission. But he did not know what lay at the end of the numbers. And he had not yet reached that end. He jogged along with his burden, heading due north and into God knew what.

# THE EXECUTIONER SERIES

# the EXECUTIONER
## TENNESSEE SMASH

# by Don Pendleton

PINNACLE BOOKS       LOS ANGELES

EXECUTIONER #32: TENNESSEE SMASH

Copyright © 1978 by Don Pendleton

An original Pinnacle Books edition, published for the first time anywhere.

ISBN: 0-523-40252-X

First Printing, April 1978

Cover illustration by Gil Cohen

Printed in the United States of America

PINNACLE BOOKS, INC.
One Century Plaza
2029 Century Park East
Los Angeles, California 90067

For Ed O'Neal, a long overdue
salute to genius.

To run true to type is the
extinction of a man, his
condemnation to death.
If . . . he is still free from
himself, he has achieved
an atom of immortality.
—Boris Pasternak (Dr. Zhivago)


Things do not change;
we change.
—Henry David Thoreau


The question is not am I
changing, but how. Death
is the final change.
—Mack Bolan, the Executioner

# TENNESSEE SMASH

# PROLOGUE

The big man in black stood in silent contemplation of the muted sounds of the city by night and the sluggish rhythms of Ol' Man River—the mighty Mississippi—as it flowed behind him with its ghostly murmurings from eternity.

Eternal, yeah . . . that was the word. A flowing stream was like the life of a moving man—eternal, yet ever changing, the waters flowing from some unseen beginning and hurrying toward an unimaginable infinity—nothing ever fixed, nothing ever certain—yet eternal . . . eternal.

Banks and beds do not a river make; Bolan knew that. Nor did waters. $H_2O$—big deal—molecules in great numbers, clinging to one another through chemical bonds while slowly drifting from nowhere to nowhere.

Like a man's life, yeah.

So where did either get such grand ideas about *eternity*? What is a river if it isn't banks and beds, hydrogen and oxygen mixed together and flowing from nowhere to nowhere? What is a man if not blood and bones, electricity and tissue mixed together and growing from nothing to nothing?

The question was purely academic. Bolan already had his answer. Both a man and a river are *events* in space and time. *Infinite* events, overflowing space and confounding time . . . thus, sure, eternal.

Ol' Man Eternal River . . . murmurs from outside space and beyond time.

Bolan shivered and shook himself to break the mood. It was no time to be thinking beyond eternity. There was work to be done, *events* to be set into motion.

It was time to put the spur to a certain aspect of the flow of life within this historic old city. Bolan knew how to do that.

He angled icy eyes for a quick and final glimpse of the stony ramparts marking Confederate Park while tossing a mental salute toward that symbol of human heroism and sacrifice. Then he spun about on softshod feet and became a living part of the eternal night.

Yes, proud Memphis—"Place of Good Abode" —Mack Bolan knew how and where to put the spurs.

# CHAPTER 1

# THE SPUR

He was rigged for soft penetration—clad in black skintights, lightly armed with the silent Beretta as head weapon, a Crossman air pistol, stiletto and garrotes—hands and face blackened for maximum invisibility.

The target was a nondescript warehouse, undistinguished from the many others in this active riverport, squatting gloomily in the deep darkness of the witching hour. A feeble luminescence glowed dimly from dirtied windows at the upper level; a naked yellow bulb outside the office door provided a small area of minimal relief from the inky night. To all outward appearances, *Delta Importers* was slumbering like most others in the Port of Memphis.

Mack Bolan knew better.

He moved in on the target as a soundless extension of the night, combat senses flaring through the atmospheres of that enemy turf in an effort to encompass all that might be lying there in wait. The lone security guard was an easy take. Bolan found him in his rounds, at the back corner of the building. He kissed him quietly with a silent dart from the Pellgun and left him there in tranquil sleep.

So far, so good—but the man in black grimaced as he consulted the wrist chronometer. It was to be a tight mission, with everything riding on the proper fall of the numbers.

Out over the river a nightbird called softly and dipped in flight to follow the track of an unwary prey. Eastward, the hushed sprawl of the city sent neon advertisements to form a faint aura overhead; but here all was blackness.

Bolan knelt motionless at the wall of the building, eyes intent upon the wrist—watching the numbers fall. He was not at all comfortable with this mission—not sure, even, in its very concept. But . . . it was committed, now. He sent a quick flick of the eyes northward as though they would perhaps reveal what the ears had not—wondering, as he did so, if he were the biggest fool alive.

No, he was not at all comfortable.

And perhaps he would not be the biggest fool *alive* for very long. But the moment had arrived and he was stuck with it. It was not a time for doubts. So he brushed the doubts aside and pushed off to follow his numbers to their uncertain conclusion.

The roof was a cinch. He gained it with a

bound, a swing, and a soft wriggle—then went on without pause to the skylight, which mission briefing had assured him would be another cinch. It was not. The wooden framing was rotted and swollen, threatening to dissolve in his hands at first touch. He went to work at the heavy glass with his stiletto, easing it out inch by breathless inch, until there was sufficient purchase with the bare hands to lift it clear.

Hell yawned up at him from that black hole.

According to the blueprints, it would be a twelve-foot drop to the floor of a storage loft—empty, supposedly. That would have been a cinch, also, if he could have lowered himself by hand to drop free the remainder of the relatively short distance. The rotten wood foreclosed that idea.

So this was where it really got ticklish.

He opted to risk the penlight for a quick flash into those depths. The loft was empty, right—but it looked more like fifteen feet than twelve, and there was no way to determine the strength of that dusty flooring.

The decision came with typical swiftness.

Bolan dropped to a crouch and pushed off with one hand, knees almost touching the chest as he dropped through the opening in the roof and entered free fall. Fifteen feet, yeah. The touchdown came with a bit more impact and noise than he was willing to settle for, even using knees and ankles to maximum cushioning effect. The old flooring swayed and groaned under the sudden weight—but it held—and Bolan whispered a thanks to kindly providence as he upholstered the Beretta and moved softly to the door.

He held there, frozen, ears straining for sign of reaction from below. Frozen moments, held together by the beating of his heart and the certain knowledge that all hearts stop beating sooner or later, for one reason or another, despite all efforts to the contrary.

He was inside a Mob powder factory.

If the intel was accurate, a full crew of chemists were at that moment busily refining and packaging a large shipment of raw heroin from Central America—under the watchful eyes of at least a dozen heavy torpedoes under one Dandy Jack Clemenza, reputed new heroin king of the Western Hemisphere.

The shipment which had arrived that very day was said to have a value of 22 million dollars after Clemenza's chemists finished stepping on it—and the streets were said to be hungry for the stuff.

So, sure, it was a big day in Memphis. And Bolan had no illusions whatever concerning the "security" for the affair, despite the easy look outside. According to the intel, each of Dandy Jack's hardmen would be toting automatic weapons and the boss himself would be right there until the last bag was sealed and the re-shipment completed.

So much for all that. Apparently none had heard Bolan's heavy entrance. He easily defeated the locking mechanism of the flimsy door and moved quietly onto the open loft. Below and directly across from his position was the area of major activity, the proceedings taking place in semidarkness and stealthy silence. Several long tables supported a surprisingly professional-looking array of laboratory equipment—bunsens, beakers, the whole bit. Ten white-coated men wearing filter masks manned the "laboratory" while in the background of semidarkness faceless stoics hovered in business suits and casually dangling submachine guns.

Clemenza himself sat at a table at the end of the line—weighing, packaging, and labelling the precious finished product.

The only light in the place was that provided at the tables—a small high intensity lamp for each of the chemists, plus two for the boss.

No one talked, except in grunts and monosyllables concerning the business at hand. Bolan counted eight gunners—and wondered if there were more and where they might be. The gossip placed them at an even dozen—but of course those things were often exaggerated.

He stood in frozen silence and watched his numbers tumbling away into infinite nowhere, looking for a handle and hoping for a miracle. Ten minutes moved like hours as he watched and waited, then fifteen . . . and then came the handle. One of the chemists raised his head and said something in a muffled grunt to Clemenza. The heroin king snapped a reply heavy with displeasure. The guy got up and walked away, the filter still in place over his nose and mouth. A gunner fell in behind the guy. Both disappeared at the edge of darkness. Bolan heard a toilet flush moments later.

And, yeah, there was the handle.

He watched the two reappear and take their places, then he made his move—maneuvering cautiously down the creaky stairway and blending quietly into the deeper shadows as he made his way across the no man's land and into the lighter area across the way.

The toilet was a mere closet, set into the corner of the building, forward. The door was latticed and the yellowish light filtering through was just enough to serve as a beacon to those in need in the darkness.

The man in black had a need of his own. He took a tactical position in the darkness and settled in to wait the need of others.

The wait was not so long, this time. Bolan had barely settled in when footsteps approached—two pair, moving casually—then a white coat materialized in the escaped light from the toilet—a tall, skinny guy—mask removed from the hawkish face and riding the throat. Right on his heels was the armed keeper, a real ironman complete with scowl and swagger.

"What's the matter with that guy?" the chemist growled quietly. "When you gotta, you gotta. Right?"

"The man is always right," replied the other—the voice flat, utterly devoid of emotion. "What you tell me, you're telling him."

They'd come to a halt, not an arm's length removed from Mack Bolan.

"I just meant—"

"He's right. You should shit on your own time. What's the beef? He told you okay, didn't he? So okay." Emotion crept in then. "Do it. And don't take all night."

The man in the white coat sneered and went on to the toilet. The guy with the burper slung the piece at his shoulder and went for a cigarette—probably as glad for the break as the other guy.

Bolan waited for the lighter to flare, then said very quietly, from about three feet out, "Hold the light, eh?"

Those startled eyes flared in double-take and the guy choked on the inhalation as he tried to do too many things with too little time. The lighter dropped toward the floor, both hands fought the other over the strap of the burper, the glowing cigarette fell into the jacket, and the guy never got his breath back. A hand of real iron crushed the fragile windpipe as another bent the spine into an impossible contortion. He was a dead man even before his lighter reached the floor—and both man and submachine gun were over the Bolan shoulder and moving quickly into the blackness of the warehouse before the man in the toilet could remove his white coat.

The corpse was stashed and the Executioner was at the door as the coat was coming off. The guy never saw what had come for him. A two-hand chop at either side of the neck sat the guy down and shuttered the eyes without so much as a gasp of understanding.

Bolan tugged the coat back into position and secured the sash, then hoisted the unconscious man to his shoulder. Satisfied, now, that the most direct route was the best route, he headed straight for the front door, threw the double bolts, and stepped into the little security room which marked the final obstacle to a successful mission.

The guy in the room had both feet on the desk, a Schmeisser one lunge away. Both feet crashed to the floor as he tried for it—a mere heartbeat removed from instant fame and glory, but a heartbeat too late.

The Beretta spat once from the doorway, chugging its silent skullbuster toward a bone-shattering denial of fame and glory. The guy fell back into the chair and stayed there, the broken head slumped limply over the backrest.

Bolan rolled chair and all into the darkened interior of the building, then got the hell out of there with his prisoner. As he rejoined the night, he knew that it had been a successful mission. But he did not know what lay at the end of the numbers. And he had not yet reached that end. He jogged along with his burden, heading due north and into God knew what.

He still was not comfortable with this mission.

He still did not know what lay beyond the mission numbers. One thing he knew for sure, though. Whoever wore the spurs, Dandy Jack Clemenza was in for a decidedly undandy night. And that was enough right there to make the whole thing worthwhile.

Even if it should turn out that the spurs were into Bolan as well.

## CHAPTER 2

## THE RIDERS

The rendezvous point was a thousand feet due north of *Delta Importers*. The site was a ramshackle building awaiting demolition.

The nuttiest part of all was that Bolan did not know whom to expect to find there. There were no lights, no sounds of life about the place. He halted at twenty feet out and lowered his burden to the ground as he softly called out, "Okay, here's your package."

A shadow figure detached itself from the side of the building and moved slowly forward.

Bolan growled, "That's far enough."

The figure halted. A small flashlight came on to illuminate the face of "Young David" Ecclefield.

He was honcho of a federal task force operating out of Atlanta—or, at least, that had been his role several Bolan lifetimes ago. They

13

had worked together then, quietly, as obviously they were doing now.

Bolan sighed and called over, "This has to be clean, David. Just the way I set it up."

"It's clean," came the strained reply. "You have the goods?"

"I have the goods," Bolan assured the fed. The guy started to move forward again. Bolan halted him with a tight: "Stay there. Pick it up when you see my back, not before. Here's a scouting report. It's exactly the way the briefing called it. Except I count only nine gunners. Two of those have been scratched."

"You agreed—"

"I agreed to keep it as soft as possible. That's as soft as it would go. There's a Pinkerton or something out back, sleeping off a tranquilizer. You'd best count on two or three gunners concealed somewhere on board with automatics."

"Okay. Thanks." The voice was wry, strained. "What about Dandy Jack?"

"He's there."

"You're sure you have the goods?"

"I'm sure," Bolan said quietly. "There should be enough powder on this guy's clothing to make a dozen cases. That's the idea, isn't it?"

"That's the idea," Ecclefield replied, sighing. "Wait!—I have a late request."

"I'm waiting."

"Someone wants to talk to you. Someone high. They're on their way now. Can you wait a few more minutes?"

"I can," Bolan said. "But you can't. They'll
14

be missing this guy and the other two. You have no numbers to waste."

"Well I—"

"I'll withdraw. Take your goods and seal it good. I'll be around. Tell your VIPs to show themselves. I'll find them."

The fed tossed him a little salute. Bolan faded to a tactical holding point and watched from the enshrouding darkness as two guys swept around Ecclefield and hurried over to the fallen prisoner. They hefted the chemist between them and quickly bore him away.

Ecclefield stood there for a moment longer, staring quietly toward the point where Bolan had stood. Then he turned abruptly and followed the others.

So. It had worked out okay, despite all the misgivings. Less than five minutes had elapsed since the purloined chemist requested permission to use the toilet. As intent as all those people had been in their business, it seemed unlikely that anyone would immediately begin to wonder about the time.

Bolan knew that fifty heavily armed federal marshals were waiting somewhere out there in the darkness—and this fact had given him the greatest pause. Bolan himself was the most wanted man in the country. Therefore he did not casually accept temporary truces with the police establishment. Regardless of who was wearing the badge, there was always that possibility. . . . Even Ecclefield had not proven himself 100 percent reliable in Bolan's eyes—though certainly the blitzer would have felt much better about the operation from the start if he had known who would be running it.

Besides the SWAT-type marshals waiting out there, Bolan knew also that there would be a special van carrying a couple of official chemists and a federal judge. They were going for broke this time. Probable cause, search warrants, the whole bit—they meant to bust Clemenza in the act and they meant to make it stand up in court. The thing had been pitched to Bolan by Hal Brognola himself—the nation's top cop—which gave an indication of how badly they wanted Dandy Jack. Even so, Bolan had been a bit surprised to find Ecclefield running the show. He had expected to find a team of cloak-and-dagger Narcs. Of course, they wanted Clemenza for many more social outrages than dealing in dope. One handle was probably as good as another, if it would put the guy on ice for a few years.

But Bolan had felt all along that there was more to this operation than he'd been told.

And now he was awaiting some sort of *tete à tete* with a couple of exotics—from Wonderland, probably.

He sensed movements in the darkness—stealthy, purposeful—and knew that the hit teams were already moving into position against *Delta Importers*.

He tossed them a mental *God keep* and wondered how much longer he had to wait around. The deal with Brognola was that Bolan would be clear and running free before the fireworks started. If he could not *control* a situation—

16

fully, his own way—then he preferred to be apart from it. Once the firing started, there would be reactions from far and wide—police reactions, specifically. That feeling of discomfort began edging back into the Bolan gut. He put a mental mark on his chronometer, representing the outer moment for Mack Bolan on this turf. No sooner had he done that than the fireworks began: the chattering of automatic weapons away in the distance, sudden luminescence in the heavens as pyrotechnic flares lit the night, power-amplified voices wafting along in the night breezes.

It was going down.

And Bolan could see it all with his mental vision, but that was suddenly prepempted by a physical stimulation—a movement of the night, a mere shifting of shadows in the vicinity of the rendezvous point.

Working that direction in a wary circle he found his "exotics" standing stiffly in the darkness outside the shack. There were two of them, a man and a woman—a little guy wearing the threads of a rhinestone cowboy and a curvaceous blonde in a leather miniskirt and cowboy boots.

Even with the darkness and the weird costumes, Bolan recognized them instantly, from vibrations as much as anything else.

The "high ups" were none other than ethnician Tommy Anders, hottest comic in the land, and the one and only Toby Ranger—God's answer to the lonely heart in every man.

Bolan stepped into the clear and quietly declared, "Roy and Dale, I presume. Where's Trigger?"

The blonde launched herself at him in instant response. He caught her on the fly and twirled her around in a warm embrace before setting her down. "Captain Courageous in the flesh," she murmured, clinging to him. "My God, you're beautiful."

He chuckled and lightly patted her highrise bottom as he replied, "Not as beautiful as I feel. What is this? Are you soggy people my VIPs?"

Anders came forth with hand outstretched, grinning ear to ear. Bolan ignored the hand and pulled the little guy into an embrace, then stood there holding them both and beaming down at them.

"I change my vote," the girl said quietly. "Anything that beautiful is downright ugly. Good thing you've got goop on your face, Bolan. I don't think I could stand you without it."

It was sort of weird, standing there embracing two of the most dear people in his life and grinning like an idiot, while the sounds of warfare swirled through the night.

He asked, "Are you two a part of this?"

"Listen to the guy," Anders replied in mock sarcasm. "Us two is the *reason* for all this."

Toby jerked free of the embrace and said, "Don't just stand here jawing! We're sogging it, Bolan. Are you in?"

He gave her a blank look. SOG—Sensitive Operations Group—was the designation for the elite team of federal undercover cops which also included old friends Carl Lyons and Smiley Dublin. Bolan had not crossed paths with the group since Hawaii—and all he'd known at that time about their future operations was that they were "drifting west"—presumably to the Orient.

"Who's getting sogged," he asked soberly, "besides Clemenza?"

"Music City," Anders replied. "The land of good ol' boys and not so good ol' gals. The town of the living legends."

"He's trying to say Nashville," Toby put in drily. "Memphis is only the tip of the Tennessee iceberg. You kicked off the Tennessee strike, Captain Cuckoo. We thought maybe you'd like a place at the finish."

"Sorry," Bolan said, frowning. "I have urgent business elsewhere." That was not entirely true. He had just wrapped up the Arizona business when the urgent plea came in from Brognola. He'd deposited the Warwagon in a secure drop and flown directly to Memphis, arriving just hours earlier. But he had been looking toward Kansas City for some time and had planned a cruise, at least, through that area during his withdrawal from the Arizona campaign. Also—as much as he loved these people—joint operations were not really his style.

"You'd better tell him," Anders muttered to Toby Ranger.

She did not respond.

Bolan asked, "Tell him what?"

"We've lost Carl and Smiley," Anders said flatly.

Toby flared, "We're not sure about that!"

"Where'd you lose them?" Bolan asked, the voice frosted with cold emotion.

"Somewhere between Singapore and Nashville," the comic replied dismally.

"That doesn't exactly narrow the field," Bolan said.

"Nuts! They're somewhere in Nashville," Toby growled. "They hit our contact floater the moment it arrived and—"

"And that was a week ago," Anders said, horning in. "Toby is as worried as I am. She's just too damn proud to—"

"It's not pride!" she said angrily.

Bolan very quietly inquired, "What does Brognola say?"

"He called *you*, didn't he, Captain Cool?"

"He called me to Memphis. He said nothing about Carl and Smiley."

"That was *her* doing," Anders reported.

So okay, sure. Bolan understood that. It was getting to be a habit—after that first meeting in Vegas when they'd saved *his* butt—first in Detroit and then in Hawaii he'd returned the favor in spades.

But Carl Lyons was another number entirely. He and Bolan went back beyond Vegas, to that terrible period in and around Los Angeles—during a time when Carl was an L.A. city cop and Mack Bolan was just an upstart soldier boy from 'Nam with a hard-on for the Mob.

As for Smiley Dublin—ah, beauty—he could not bear to think of her as a living geek *a la* Georgette Chebleu, the first of the Ranger Girls to discover the terrifying realities of life on the edge of the knife.

Hell, there was no decision to it.

"Give me that Nashville floater," Bolan said numbly. "I'll hit it before dawn."

A tear slipped from Toby's eye and she spun angrily away to hide it.

The hottest comic in the land was not so loathe to display honest emotion. It came with the territory. Those who live largely also suffer largely. It was a highly emotional game. Tears of relief were streaming down his cheeks. He handed Bolan a card with writing on it and he said, "It's such a helpless feeling, you know. They've been missing a week. I've been walking the damn walls."

Toby cried from the background, "Oh damnit, Bolan, he set up this entire Clemenza hit. He's not so—!"

"I know what Tommy is," Bolan said coldly, cutting that off before it could be said. "He's no clown," she was telling him. Mack Bolan did not need to be told that.

"See you in Legend City," he said quietly, then very quickly got away from there.

Numbers were falling everywhere.

Police sirens were screaming through the night, converging on the riverfront. The entire area was becoming a hellground—especially for a man like Mack Bolan.

At least, now, he knew why the gut had been

21

clutching ever since his arrival in the area. And he knew, now, why he'd had the starkly spooky feeling down at river's edge, just before the pushoff.

The universe had been whispering to him.

And, yeah, Mack Bolan would go to Nashville, depend on it. Even if he had to ride the hounds of hell all the way.

# CHAPTER 3

# THE RIDDEN

Nashville is one of those small towns which virtually overnight became a major city—but never quite got into the spirit of the thing. In its heart, Nashville is still a small town though it numbers nearly half a million citizens within its borders—borders which expanded suddenly in the early sixties, at the stroke of a pen, to absorb all of surrounding Davidson County.

To most people, Nashville means country music—and though that industry alone accounts for some 60 million dollars of the city's annual economy, the music business is not the sum total of what Nashville is about. Nashville is at the heart of a major commercial, educational and cultural complex with more than fifty colleges, universities and vocational schools, some 500 manufacturers. Publishing, not "picking," is the leading industry. It is a major banking and investment center and ranks only behind Hartford, Connecticut, as the city with the most major insurance company offices.

The "Nashville Sound" has, of course, made the town second only to New York as a recording capital of the world—but culture lovers should also know that the city supports a symphony orchestra and a fine arts center. Although those latter hardly draw the crowds that flock to the $25,000,000 complex known as *Opryland USA*, they do serve notice that Nashville is a city of interesting contrasts with something for almost every taste.

And Mack Bolan had to wonder about the interests it held for the mob. Jack Grimaldi, the Mafia flyboy and secret Bolan ally, had very little to offer in that regard—despite the fact that he had been flying Syndicate bigwigs and couriers into the area for months. He'd been briefing Bolan on the area since their departure from Memphis, and now he told him, "Look straight down. That's Fort Nashborough, facing the river there. See it?"

"I see it," Bolan replied. "Any special significance?"

"Only as a historical shrine," Grimaldi said. "It's the original site of Nashville. Built about 1790, I believe."

"That long ago, eh?" Bolan asked absently.

"Yeah, just a few years after we became a nation. Andy Jackson got here before that. The guy was a horsetrader. Can you believe that?

Who the hell did he trade with before the settlers came?"

"That the same guy who became President?"

"Right. His old home is still here. It's a shrine, too. The Hermitage. Wonder why he called it that?"

"Did he name it before or after he went to Washington?" Bolan inquired lightly.

"Beats me," the pilot said, grinning. "He was the first congressman from Tennessee you know."

No, Bolan did not know that.

"First President from here, too. Tennessee has sent three of 'em. He was the first. Imagine. A horsetrader."

Bolan chuckled.

Grimaldi said, "Did you know they were pro-Union, before the war actually started? Last state to secede, first to come back in."

Yes, Bolan knew all about that particular bit of history. "Ironic, isn't it," he said softly. "This state was one of the major battlegrounds of the war. Over seven hundred battles. Second only to Virginia in battles and skirmishes fought."

"That right?"

"Yeah. General Hood met his great defeat right here at Nashville. That was one of the battles that broke the South's back. It was the only full rout of a major rebel force. Hood lost six of his generals. He wept after the battle and resigned his commission a month later."

Grimaldi shot his passenger a quick look and

commented, "You're quite a war historian, aren't you?"

"War is a science," Bolan replied quietly. "You study it if you mean to master it."

"Right, Master," the pilot said. "Airport's straight ahead. Do we go right in?"

"Fly by once and tell me how it looks, Jack. You know—from a master pilot's point of view. Let's make sure it's cool."

"Amen to that," Grimaldi said, and dipped the nose into the final descent.

At that very moment, a telephone rang in a swank townhouse not far from Nashville's Music Row. The groggy man who snapped on the bedlamp and reached for the instrument was about thirty years old, handsome, and a bit out of sorts at the moment. "Who the hell?" he growled at the caller.

The voice in the receiver was twangy, worried. "You sleeping alone, Ray?"

"Who's sleeping, damnit?"

"It's urgent—okay? I'm at a phone booth just down the street. You want to meet me or . . . ?"

The man swore softly as he turned blurry eyes toward the nude girl who lay asleep at his side. He sighed and said, "In the middle of the damn night? Can't it wait?"

"Maybe it can but it shouldn't, hoss. It really shouldn't."

The man sighed again and said with resignation, "Okay. Come on over. But keep it quiet. I got company." He hung up, scratched his head vigorously with both hands, then turned off the lamp and softly left the room.

He was drinking milk from a quart carton and nervously pacing the floor of the living room when his caller scratched at the front door.

The man who entered was a bit younger and had the lean, hard look of a gunfighter straight from the Old West. His attire was subdued "country gentleman" with the trousers stuffed casually into western boots. "Who're you sleeping with, hoss?" he asked in greeting.

"None of your damn business," said the host, but pleasantly. "What's so urgent?"

The visitor went to a chair and dropped into it with a heavy sigh. "It just came down the vine a few minutes ago. An army of federals swooped down on old Dandy tonight. They got 'im cold, buried in powder. About a ton of it, what I hear. Not even a kilo was saved. I thought you'd want to know, middle of the night or not. But it ain't. It's closer to five o'clock."

The other man was easing slowly onto the couch. He said, very softly, "Good God."

"Does that touch you, hoss?"

"What d'you mean? No! Nobody can connect us!"

"That ain't what I meant. I meant does it *touch* you. Are you laughin' or cryin' on the inside?"

"Bet your ass I'm not laughing," said the other. "How 'bout you?"

The cowboy laughed lightly and spread his

27

hands. "You know me, hoss. Easy come, easy go. I was born with nothing but a six-string geetar in my hands. I guess I can go out the same way."

"This just plays hell with everything, you know."

"That's what I said, hoss."

"A ten million dollar deal. And it won't wait for other connections. I gotta have the stuff *now*."

"You ain't gonna get it, you know."

"Well by God we'll see!"

"I'm tellin' ya, you ain't. Dandy was the *man*. He had it cornered, the whole market. When he fell, it all fell with 'im. It'd take another month even if Dandy hisself could start workin' on it. And there's only one Dandy Jack I know of, podner."

"Well goddamnit, there's *got* to be . . ."

The visitor got to his feet and said, "There ain't. That's what I come to tell ya. I don't know how far your tail is out on this deal but . . . well, hoss, you got a lot of people standin' and waitin' for this deal. If you can't deliver, then I hope you got a hole somewheres to run to. Know what I mean?"

"Wait a minute, Jess." That worried face was beginning to reflect a flickering hope. "Maybe we can still pull it out. Tell your sponsor I've got an ace in the hole. Tell him that."

"You better be damn sure before I tell him *any*thing."

"I'm sure, yeah. Pretty sure. Tell him I'm pretty sure."

28

The lean man went out chuckling at some secret joke.

The other paced the floor for several minutes then went to the bedroom and picked up the telephone.

The face was screwed into lines of painful indecision as he began dialing—then he changed his mind and put the phone back down.

The girl on the bed stirred and looked up at him. "Ooh hoo, it was great, baby," she murmured sleepily.

He gathered her clothing and dropped it in a pile beside the bed as he told her, "You're a real ball, kid. Now beat it. Party's over."

The girl picked up her clothing and staggered toward the bathroom without a word.

One party was over, for sure.

But another was just getting underway. Mack Bolan's quiet Mafia wings were at that moment lightly kissing the earth of Music City USA.

# CHAPTER 4

# SIZING IT

Bolan carried a small bag into the locker room at the private air terminal and began the Nashville transformation while pilot Grimaldi took care of the formalities at the desk. He changed into faded Levi's and Indian moccasins, nailhead shirt and denim jacket. He studied his hair for a moment, then went to work on a new look to fit the masquerade, combing it straight back from the forehead without a part, adding a streak of white through the middle, finally cementing it all in place with a heavy spray job. Purple-tinted oval glasses completed the transformation. A .38 snug Chief's Special with a high-rider waistclip holster fit snugly beneath the jacket.

He returned to the lobby and went to the telephone to leave a message on the SOG contact drop. "It's La Mancha," he told the recorder. "I'll be at the Holiday Inn for breakfast at six."

Then he stood casually at the large front window and lit a cigarette. Grimaldi completed his transactions and walked right past him enroute to the locker room. He halted suddenly, several paces beyond, and turned back with a sheepish grin overriding a questioning gaze.

Bolan chucklingly confirmed the identification and asked, "Are we set?"

The pilot ambled back to the window and stood beside the big man to tell him, "Yeah. Helicopter is usually available on an hour's notice but nothing's guaranteed. So I took a twenty-four-hour lease." He cracked his knuckles and gazed around the deserted flying service lobby. "How do you do it, guy? I saw you, but I didn't see you. It's downright spooky sometimes."

"Sleight of hand is all in the beholder, Jack," Bolan replied lightly. "The eyes take the picture but it's up to the mind to see what's really there."

Grimaldi was shooting him furtive looks. He said, "If you say so, okay. Uh—the wheels are out back. I got you an Impala. Hope that's okay."

"That's fine, yeah."

The pilot handed over the keys and rental papers. "Where can I contact you?"

Bolan said, "Check into the Ramada, downtown, and hang tight. I'll be in touch."

"That's ten to fifteen minutes from here," the Mafia flyboy groused. "I'll take the chopper

32

in. There's a place down by the river where I can leave it. Then I'll only be a couple minutes away if you should need me quick."

Bolan nodded his agreement. "So long as it doesn't compromise you, Jack."

The guy waved a hand in dismissal. "Don't worry about me. Just hold onto your own ass. If you need a liftout, just scream. I'll be there."

Bolan warmly gripped the loyal friend by the shoulder then went out of there. Strange, sometimes, the curious weavings of fate. He'd first crossed paths with Grimaldi at about the same moment as the first encounter with the SOG people. Grimaldi, while not a truly "made" man was nevertheless an employee of the crime syndicate and therefore inherently an enemy to the grave. The soggers, on the other hand, though not truly cops in the usual sense were nevertheless federal agents bent on upholding the law and serving the ends of the country's justice system—therefore just as dangerous to a guy like Bolan. That both sides of the equation were now Bolan allies was, indeed, a curious and remarkable thing.

The local Holiday Inn was grouped with several other downtown motels overlooking the state capitol grounds. Bolan strolled into the dining room at precisely six o'clock. Employees were scurrying about trying to set up for the breakfast trade and it appeared that they were not yet open for business.

Toby Ranger and Tommy Anders, though, sat with cups held casually to their lips at a window table. Nobody else was in evidence. Bolan helped himself to some coffee and carried it to the table.

"What time does it open?" he inquired, by way of greeting.

Anders looked up with a disinterested gaze and replied, "Beats me, guy. I guess it's self-serve, they got a—" He stopped talking suddenly and flashed a glance toward Toby, then laughed softly and said, "Hell, siddown. I didn't spot you right off."

Bolan slid in next to the lady and gave her a peck on the cheek.

"Watch it, Captain Hard," she muttered. "I have a quick switch and this is no time to be tripping it." Lovely eyes flashed over him. "I like your little suit. But which planet did those hairdo and purple shades come from?"

Anders commented, "It's very effective. I'm still not sure who it is."

"The name is Lambretta," Bolan said soberly. "Guys in the know call me Frankie."

"It fits," Toby said. ". . . a Madison Avenue cowboy."

"That's the idea," he told her, and turned his gaze to the comic. "Where're you working, Tom?"

"I've been doing a gig out at the new Opry. Also looking into a couple of record offers. Toby's headlining, knocking 'em dead. We been here ten days, now. Should've been on our way out by tomorrow. But it's falling to hell, so I really don't know."

A teenage boy approached the table with

water and menus. "We have a breakfast buffet," he announced. "Or the waitress will take your order in a few minutes. I recommend the buffet."

The three exchanged glances and unanimously opted for the self-serve department. Conversation was limited to small talk as they wandered to the steam table and made their selections. Bolan took scrambled eggs and bacon and carried Toby's fruit assortment to the table for her. Anders ended up with melon and tomato juice, but ate very little as the meeting got down to business.

"Tell me everything you know or think you know," Bolan demanded of his companions.

It took a bit of telling. The SOG-3 team had drifted to the Orient from Hawaii and began burrowing into the drug traffic from the Golden Triangle. It was about that time, they related, when Dandy Jack Clemenza had begun making his pitch to the collective families of Mafia for a centralized, single-source approach to America's illegal drug markets. Since the families bankrolled most of the big drug buys on an individual basis anyway, Clemenza's brainstorm was to move *en masse* to take over the entire North American operation—in an organized manner—thus cornering the entire American import market in illegal drugs. That way, they could control market prices at every level, manipulate the equation of supply and demand, and fix an iron fist upon every user and dealer in the country. Included in the scheme was a proposed national distribution

35

network which would minimize legal harassment while introducing a stability which had never been present in such operations. Distribution was, of course, the key to the whole grand plan. And it marked an extension of interests for the Mob—who, because of the inherent risks, had traditionally remained shy of actual involvement in routine trafficking.

"And this brings us to Nashville?" Bolan commented.

"In spades," Anders replied. "We think that Nashville is shaping into the national headquarters for the entire operation. We know for sure that the first trial run into national distribution will be launched from here. The smack factory in Memphis is the prime facility. There are others, bigger and better, so there has to be a good reason for selecting Memphis as processing point for the first big batch to come over. Part of the reason is Clemenza himself, of course. He's been operating through the *Delta Importers* front for over a year—but it's always been small potatoes up 'til now."

"You're saying that this new empire has not actually come into existence," Bolan observed.

Toby picked it up. "We think not yet. Apparently Clemenza is still trying to sell the idea to the collective families. That's vital, see. Either they all come in or the whole idea falls apart. Competition would kill it. The shipment we knocked over last night was to have served as the proof run."

"We weren't trying to kill it," Anders explained. "Just divert it a bit. If the thing looks good to the Families, they'll pick it up with or without Clemenza. We want them to pick it up."

Sure they did. The SOGs had a lot more in mind than the simple harassment of drug traffickers. They wanted what Mack Bolan wanted. They wanted an end to organized crime in America.

"So why did you knock over Clemenza?" Bolan wondered aloud.

"Because we had a replacement standing in the wings," Anders quietly replied.

Bolan sighed. "Lyons, eh."

"Right. But we're calling him Carl Leonetti, these days. He met Clemenza in Singapore last month while the guy was firming up the supply lines."

"Is there a real Carl Leonetti?"

"Used to be. He died of yellow fever ten years ago in Indonesia, at the age of fifteen. He was the only son of Roberto Leonetti who died in the Brooklyn wars a few years ago. The kid was on a hasty world cruise with his mother. They both got the fever and died. Actually they were on the lam from Leonetti's troubles in New York. Somebody in the State Department neglected to pass the word to Roberto. He probably died thinking the lady took the kid and skipped out on him. Everybody in the Mob, back then, knew that he was scouring the world for them—very quietly, of course. Leonetti had a lot of enemies."

Bolan said, "Yeah." The story was coming

back to him, now. "So Carl Lyons becomes the long-missing Carl Leonetti. Go on."

Toby said, "Clemenza liked his credentials and signed him on as his agent and courier in the Far East. It was Carl who brought in the major part of the stuff we seized last night."

Anders added, "By way of South America."

Toby continued, "But he also brought quite a bit more than he delivered. That's the story, anyway. We were setting him up, see, as an alternate to Dandy Jack."

"Good plan," Bolan mused. "What went wrong?"

Anders spread his hands in a gesture of puzzlement and replied with misery in the voice. "We just don't know. Smiley's traveling with him, too, as his wife and assistant. We dredged up a foolproof identity for her, too. She's a White Russian, a granddaughter of some refugees from the revolution. There's lots of them there. She died, too, awhile back—natural causes—but the records don't show it."

Toby said, "They arrived in Nashville right on schedule and left the message on our floater. Carl said that he was already set up with a meeting, to be held that evening, with some "future associates" of Clemenza. And that's the last we've heard."

"You have no idea who he was meeting?"

Anders shook his head. "Neither did he, apparently. We do know that Clemenza's main man in Nashville is a guy going by the name of Oxley—Ray Oxley—real name Raymond Accimentio. He's the figurehead of an outfit called

38

Roxy Artists Management, Inc. We've had the guy under day and night surveillance for the better part of a week. Nothing. Absolutely nothing."

Bolan asked, "How many people are working this with you?"

The two exchanged troubled glances. "There's a bunch," Toby said quietly.

"Call them all in," Bolan suggested. "Clear the field. I don't want to be playing the friend-or-foe routine."

Toby said to Anders, "I told you he'd just waltz in and take it all over."

Anders grinned feebly at Bolan and said, "We've been working this for a long time, buddy. We'd hate to see it all blow up now."

Bolan sighed. "It's already blown up, hasn't it? You've got Clemenza on ice and his powders off the market. Without Lyons, you've got no show. Tell all your people to get lost for twenty-four hours. If I'm not back with Carl and Smiley by then, well—then you'll know they won't be getting back. Meanwhile you need to be looking at your options, don't you? One more question. Where does David Ecclefield fit into your operation? Last I saw the guy he was running strike forces in Atlanta."

"He's not doing that any more," was all Toby said.

Bolan was giving the frosty gaze to Tommy Anders. The little comic fidgeted uncomfortably for a moment, then said, "What the hell, Toby—we don't keep secrets from this guy." The gaze shifted to a square fit with Bolan's.

"David has joined the game. He's domestic operations chief. It's a support outfit. Okay?"

Bolan smiled without humor as he replied, "Okay. Give him my respects. And tell him to keep his support out of my way for the next twenty-four hours."

"You're blitzing," Toby Ranger said with a sigh.

"Is there any other way?" Bolan quietly inquired.

For reply she leaned into him and snaked both arms around his neck, melting against him with a soulful kiss.

Anders, on the sidelines, chuckled softly as he commented, "There, damn ya. Now go out there and conquer Music City."

And Mack Bolan knew that he would have to do precisely that.

# CHAPTER 5

# SPEAK FEAR

"Good morning, Mr. Oxley."

The *macho* young president of Roxy Artists Management Inc. swept past the pretty receptionist without acknowledging the greeting. Nervous hopefuls clutching guitars and demo records overflowed the large outer office. He gave these a quick, measuring glance as he rounded the corner and entered the corridor to the private offices.

It was business as usual on this most extraordinary, unreal day. All of the glass-fronted audition booths were occupied and the agents' cubicles were humming with a dozen conversations as Oxley ran the gauntlet to his sanctorum. At any other time it would have been music to his ears; today he was thankful for the soundproofed private suite.

The hubbub disappeared behind the closed

41

door as he moved briskly inside and greeted his secretary.

"It's off and running early, isn't it?"

"Yes, sir. And there's—"

"I don't want to be disturbed, Doris. No calls, no visitors, no exceptions."

The woman's eyes revealed an inner worry. "I'm sorry. You already have a visitor. He's waiting inside. Simply would not take no for an answer. The men weren't in yet so I decided I'd better just—I think he's from . . . from . . . you know."

Yes, damnit, Oxley knew, or thought he did. And it was not a total surprise. He hid the displeasure from his secretary while telling her, "Soon as Arthur and Jimbo get in, tell them to hang close." He arched an eyebrow at her. "I'm liable to need them."

But that was just for show. The men were the best legbreakers in town, sure. But this was no time for mere legbreakers—not if Oxley's hunch was on target.

It was.

The visitor was a total stranger—big guy, neatly dressed in denims, purple lenses shading the eyes. The atmosphere in the room was almost electric. Oxley suppressed an inner tremor as he pushed on inside and carefully closed the door.

The guy was standing by the window in semi-profile with the morning light behind him. The face was therefore not too clear but Oxley knew instinctively that he did not know this man. The *type*, yeah . . . okay. Oxley knew immediately what the guy *was*. But he had not anticipated the greeting he got.

"Are you Raymond Accimentio?" inquired the cold voice from the window.

Oxley went on to his desk. He sat down, lit a cigarette and toyed with a paperweight as his mind spun through the situation. What the hell *was* this? The guy had *hitman* written all over him. Surely things had not gone that sour that fast. But it was the standard hitman greeting. They hated to make mistakes. They liked to know for sure. *Are you the guy I've been sent to burn?*

The troubled man took a deep pull at the cigarette and cautiously replied, "I haven't used that name for a long time. You know who I am. What's the game?"

"It's called 'kiss your ass goodbye'," was the cold response.

Oxley had not been aware of a flicker of movement over there, but suddenly an ugly snubnosed pistol was yawning on him.

He froze with the cigarette pointed toward an ashtray as a million and a half thoughts careened through his mind. His heart went into triple-time. His mouth was suddenly very dry, the tongue overlarge and threatening to seal off his throat. His voice, when it came, was weak and raspy. "Now wait! This is . . . misunderstanding! We can straighten it out!"

"You can't raise the dead, *amici*," said the big frigid man.

"What's that supposed to mean?" Oxley squawked. "I'm not—I didn't—who's dead?"

"You are," said the voice of doom. "It's tit for tat, Raymond. So kiss it goodbye."

"This is a terrible mistake!" Oxley yelled. He staggered to his feet and leaned weakly back against the desk, both hands held out in a loose boxing stance at chest level. This was the most terrifying moment of his life. Things like this didn't really *happen*—did they? But, yes, that son of a bitch meant business for sure! "It's crazy! You got the wrong guy! I don't even know what you're talking about!"

The man at the window had not moved. He said, "We're talking about Carl Leonetti."

"Who?"

"And Dandy Jack Clemenza. That was no way to honor a deal."

Oh for God's sake! Oxley giggled in near hysteria, overjoyed with a sudden understanding. It *was* a gruesome mistake! "Hey, buddy—*amici!*—you got it all wrong! Clemenza's not dead! He took a fall, that's all! I had nothing to do with that, for God's sake! I thought at first you were from the *other* people! God! Scared the *shit* outta me, you did. *Those* people are the ones I'm worried about! They got a big investment in this. Naturally—I mean I'd expect them to be worried about their investment. I thought you were from *them*. Hey!—I'm with Clemenza all the way on this thing. What hurts him, hurts me. You got it all wrong."

The purple shades came away from that impassive face. Oxley felt impaled by probing blue eyes—penetrated, examined, judged and sealed. Finally: "Is that all you have to say?"

"No! I never met Leonetti. I know he's with Clemenza on this, too, but we never met. He hit town last week. We talked on the phone. I set up his contact and that's all. I never saw him."

"Who burned him, then?"

"God I didn't know he got burned. I was hoping to find him, myself. I figure he's my only out. I need the product and I need it bad. Like I said, there's this big investment. I got to deliver on that investment. Who burned him?"

The big guy seemed to be giving Oxley a second inspection. Then, that cold voice again: "Send for your leg-breakers."

"What?"

"The two Swedish Angels—Jimbo and Arthur. Call them in here."

Oxley was greatly confused by the command but he gladly leaned over the intercom and obeyed it.

Thank God they were there.

The two bruisers were at the door before Oxley could straighten up. They came in cautiously and halted just inside the room, obviously sensitized by the heavy atmosphere.

The guy at the window said to them, "Let's come to an understanding, boys." He was putting the gun away. The fucking idiot! Oxley was breathing better already. "I just want one thing. I want my partner, Carl Leonetti. So let's decide where he is and let me be on my way."

Like shit!

Jimbo shot an oblique and loaded gaze at his

boss while Arthur took on the cold stare of the visitor.

"Relax," said Oxley with an easy laugh. "There was a misunderstanding but it's straightened out, now. Mr. uh . . . mister . . . ?"

The guy at the window supplied the name with no change in voice tones. "Lambretta. Call me Frankie."

"Oh right, sure. Frankie is worried about his partner, boys. If you know anything about a man named Carl Leonetti, now's the time to spit it out."

Arthur had no patience for games of finesse. His massive shoulders were hunched forward and the fingers of both hands were splayed and flexing. "You want me to toss this hotshot outta here, Mr. Oxley?" he rumbled.

"No no," Oxley replied grandly, enjoying the moment. "It's cool. I told you to relax. Let's give the man his answers before we throw him out."

"I got no answers," Arthur growled.

"Me neither," seconded Jimbo.

"There you go," Oxley said sweetly to his visitor. "Both of these boys are armed, of course. But I'm sure they'd rather break you open with their hands. I guess you have that much choice."

But that was a mistake. As it turned out, the big guy at the window apparently had infinite choices in the matter. Both of the bodyguards were going for their weapons when the snub-nose magically leapt into Lambretta's hand, seemingly roaring as it did so. Arthur was flung backward with a gaping well between the eyes. Jimbo's mouth exploded into a crimson fountain, the eyes twitching and rolling momentarily as he crumpled to the floor.

Oxley's ears were ringing from the twin explosions. He was stunned, ill and terrified all at once. His vision was going in and out and he could see Lambretta now as only a red-tinted shadow occupying a halo of light—still at the window. Then Oxley realized that the red tints were being produced by human blood dripping from his forehead—Jimbo's blood—and the smell of it was overpowering his senses.

He heard his own voice pleading eerily from the background of horror as the image at the window began moving closer. The dissociated groveling sickened him even further, but he could not control it.

He was on his knees, for God's sake, in Jimbo's blood, begging for mercy!

And the big man was standing over him now, the hot muzzle of the pistol at Oxley's forehead.

"You're naked now," the cold voice told him, from somewhere atop the red halo. "You're better off that way, so stay there. No more games. No more cute. We'll talk now, Raymond."

And, of course, they did.

Yes. They really got down to the talking, then.

# CHAPTER 6

# DEATH LOGIC

"Don't do it! Please! Anything you want . . . whatever . . . just say it!"

"I told you what I want, Raymond."

"I never met the guy! I talked to him on the phone! That's all!"

"And when was that?"

"About a week ago. It was last Tuesday."

"Why did you talk to him?"

"Huh? He called me."

"What about?"

"Well he was—I knew who he was. I mean I knew the name. He brought in some product for Dandy Jack. He said he was worried about that. He didn't like Dandy's operation. He said he had a fail-safe and he wanted to talk to somebody about that."

"He had a what?"

"I figured he meant another shipment, a product reserve."

"And what did you say?"

"I said it wasn't part of the deal. I told him I couldn't even talk to him about that. That wasn't my territory."

"What *is* your territory?"

"Uh ... I'm more on the distribution side."

"Street distribution."

"No, no. National distribution."

"This is where it starts?"

"Yeah."

"How?"

"Huh?"

"How?"

"Uh ... well we have a natural setup here. You know, we send people all over the country. From here. Also a lot of promo and demo material."

"Uh huh."

"Perfect setup, isn't it?"

"Yeah it's quite a setup, Raymond. So why didn't you want to deal with Carl? Product is product, isn't it?"

"Well, no. He had raw stuff. That's Dandy's territory . . . the raw stuff. He has to step on it before I get it. I can't handle raw product. Anyway it sounded like double dealing and it scared me. I couldn't get involved in anything like that."

"You wouldn't get involved like that."

"Hell no. That would be stepping outside. I wouldn't think of stepping outside. That's very dangerous, you know. A guy could end up at the bottom of the Cumberland in a cement barrel."

"So you turned Carl over to the cement men, eh?"

"No! I swear I didn't do that! I just told him I couldn't afford to get involved but I could pass him on up to the right people. He explained, see, and then I realized I'd gotten the wrong impression. He wasn't trying to double deal. He was just trying to fail-safe it in case something went sour with Dandy . . . and that's what he was worried about."

"But you didn't want to get involved in that either."

"Well it was over my head, see. I'm just a cog in this machine. I explained that to Leonetti. He understood. He thanked me."

"Thanked you for what?"

"For helping him get lined up."

"How did you do that?"

"I told you. I passed him to the right people."

"Who did you pass him to?"

"Huh?"

"Who did you pass him to?"

"To uh . . . I passed him to my sponsor."

"What does that mean?"

"That means the people I report to."

"You're mixing singular and plural, Raymond. How many people did you pass him to?"

"I passed him to my sponsor."

"Singular or plural?"

"Oh, that's plural."

"You're not being much help, Raymond."

"No, look! Wait now! I'm not trying to

screw you around! I'm just trying to explain it!"

"Try a little harder."

"Look, see, I'm president of this company."

"Okay."

"I'm the chief executive officer. But God, I don't *own* it."

"Who does?"

"Well, a lot of people are involved. I don't even know who all is involved. I report to Nick Copa."

"Nick who?"

"Copa. That's C-O-P-A. He's the controller. I mean, he's the local owning partner."

"Well now, exactly what is he, Raymond? Is he the controller or is he an owner?"

"Both. He's both. He's the local—the on-scene controller for the owning corporation. He has partners all over the country."

"Like who?"

"Oh hell, I don't know that. They don't tell me that."

"And you never wonder about it, eh?"

"Sure, I wonder. I wonder a lot."

"Do some wondering now, Raymond."

"Huh? Oh. Okay. We have this deal with *TeleBoost*. I think that's one of their satellite companies."

"What is *TeleBoost*?"

"They do special promotions. You know. Publicity. To get our artists some national exposure."

"Keep on wondering."

"Then there's *Emcee*. They get—"

52

"What is *Emcee*?"

"That's a recording label. A record company. *Emcee Records*. They specialize in golden packaging and TV sales."

"Run that by me again."

"Selling by mail order. You've seen those ads on television. Like that."

"This isn't helping, Raymond."

"Okay, okay, hold it! It's hurting my head. The gun is hurting. Okay?"

"It's going to keep on hurting until I get something more than your corporate family tree."

"I'm trying to explain it. Okay? The same men own all these companies. See? They also own hotels and casinos and night clubs and all that. And they got a hundred or more company names. How the hell would I know who owns what? How would anybody? Nick Copa is the only guy I ever see. He's the Nashville controller. For the company. For the whole umbrella of companies."

"You also called him a partner."

"In a sense, yes, he's a partner."

"In what sense?"

"In the sense that in Nashville Nick Copa is the boss."

"Boss of what?"

"Of everything I've been talking about."

"But he's nationally connected."

"Oh sure."

"What's the Family?"

"Uh, God, I don't know. Don't ask me that. Even if I knew, I couldn't . . ."

"New York?"

"Maybe New York. Maybe Chicago. I don't know. I don't even think it's a family group—not like a *family*, you know. More like a coalition. It's a corporation in the national sense."

"Based in New York or Chicago?"

"Maybe both, maybe neither, I just don't know. Can I get up? All this blood is making me sick to my stomach. I've got to get—"

"Not yet, Raymond. You stay there and keep thinking. Did you put Carl in touch with Nick Copa?"

"Oh no, God no. I wouldn't even *think* of . . ."

"Who, then?"

"I never initiate direct contact with Nick. If he wants me, he lets me know. But I never initiate anything."

"Who, Raymond?"

"There's this guy . . . works for Nick . . . *directly* for Nick . . ."

"Sort of a lieutenant."

"Like that, yeah. I passed your friend to this guy."

"How did you do that?"

"Leonetti says he'll be at such and such a place at such and such a time. I tell him that's fine, I'll pass the word on where'll he be."

"And?"

"And I did."

"Who did you pass it to?"

"I passed it to this lieutenant."

"This lieutenant has a name?"

"Uh, sure, he has a name. They call him Gordy, I think."

54

"What else do they call him?"

"Uh, I think his name is Mazzarelli."

"Gordy Mazzarelli."

"Yeah."

"Say it, Raymond. Say it right out. What is this lieutenant's name?—this lieutenant you passed Carl to?"

"Gordy Mazzarelli, I said it. Didn't I say it?"

"You called Gordy Mazzarelli and you told Gordy Mazzarelli that Carl Leonetti would be in such a place at such a time."

"That's right."

"What else did you tell Gordy Mazzarelli?"

"That's all I told him."

"So of course Gordy already knew who Carl Leonetti is."

"Well I guessed he did."

"Uh huh."

"But of course I told him why he called."

"Uh huh."

"I told him about this fail-safe supply."

"What else?"

"I told him that Leonetti was trying to sell— wanted to talk to someone in the company about that supply."

"And what did Gordy say?"

"Huh?"

"What did Gordy say about Carl wanting to talk to someone?"

"He said okay."

"Okay what?"

"Okay, he'd meet him."

"Who said that?"

"Gordy said that. Gordy Mazzarelli said

okay he'd meet him. He'd meet Leonetti and discuss it with him."

"Look at my other hand, Raymond. See this? Know what this is?"

"Looks like a—what the hell? Have you been taping this?"

"All the way. Know why?"

"No I don't know why."

"You don't care?"

"No, I don't care."

"Maybe Gordy would care."

"Hey, don't even, uh. . . . You wouldn't. . . ."

"Call it a fail-safe, Raymond. I'll let Gordy listen to the tape and I'll give him the same option I've given you."

"Please don't do that!"

"Don't do what?"

"Don't let Gordy know I fingered him!"

"Why not? If all they did was meet and talk. . . ."

"You know what I mean! Even if they were long lost brothers and I brought them back together, you know the position I'm in talking to you like this! You've got to keep this confidential!"

"It won't matter, Raymond. When I'm done with Gordy—"

"No, you don't understand! You don't know what you're going against! I do, I know! You don't stand a chance. This guy is Nick Copa's personal torpedo—plus a whole goddamn crew of crazies! You don't stand a chance!"

"That's why I made the tape. You're going

to even out the odds a bit for me. You're going to give me every possible edge, aren't you?"

"I don't—how can I? What—?"

"You're tied to me, Raymond. In life or in death. There's only one logic for you now, guy. How do you want to play it?"

"I want to play it far away from Crazy Gordy. Let's just keep him out of this."

"I guess that's your decision."

"Yeah. I see what you mean. Okay, look. I don't know what they did with Leonetti. I know that he caused quite a stir. I passed him on and that's all I know. Never a word came back. But I know where his woman is. I'll make a deal. You give me that tape. I'll tell you where the woman is. Maybe she knows something."

Bolan had a better deal in mind.

"Let's go find the lady, first. Then we'll talk a deal. If there's anything left to deal for."

"And what if there isn't?"

"Then we'll seal that deal in hell, guy."

"I'll help all I can," Oxley whispered, sighing in final defeat. It was the raw fear of death speaking, in its own pure logic.

And Mack Bolan knew that it spoke the truth.

It spoke, also, of the stretch toward life. And that was a logic of another kind.

# CHAPTER 7

# ONCE SOFTLY

It was a wooded estate enclosed by a stone wall. A cluster of red tile roofs poked through the treetops deep within. A modest, dull bronze signboard on the gatepost identified the place as the Juliana Academy and a hastily painted shingle forbade unauthorized entry. The gate was mechanized and operated by remote control from somewhere within. No other security protections were in evidence.

The portion of the grounds visible from the gate was in neglect. Grass and weeds had encrouched upon the drive from both sides. Fallen debris from trees littered the entire area. The wall itself was crumbling, here and there.

According to Oxley, the place had once been a school for girls. Now it was the center of activities for a farflung prostitution ring. Oxley still referred to it as "the school" and had said that he often "referred" young female artists here as a friendly place to improve performing skills while waiting for a break. Bolan knew all too well the only kind of break a girl could expect from a setup like this.

He aligned his vehicle into the entry slot and pushed a button on the call box. He had to send the signal twice again before a crisp female voice responded.

"State your name and business, please."

Bolan growled back at the box, "Lambretta. Errand for Mr. Copa. Come on, shake it. I ain't got all day."

The gate opened without further ado. He eased the car inside and made a slow approach along the drive, alertly taking the lie of the place. There were three buildings all in a cluster about two hundred yards inside the grounds. The architecture was Mediterranean and it had obviously once been beautiful. The central building was a three-story structure with outside staircases and crumbling patios. The flanking structures were large but single stories, rambling—also showing signs of decay and neglect.

A guy was waiting for him outside the main building. He had the Music Row look but Bolan knew better. He stopped the car and got out, scowling not at the greeter but at the shabby buildings.

"Great old joint," he said coldly. "Why the hell don't you fix it up?"

"Why the hell should *I* fix it up, hoss?" the guy drawled.

"What'd you call me?" Bolan growled.

The man grinned and held both hands out at shoulder level. "No offense. It's just my way of being friendly. "What *should* I call you?"

"*You* should call me Mr. Lambretta."

The cowboy laughed lightly and replied, "So that's what I'll call you. What can I do for you, sir?"

Bolan lit a cigarette while still looking the place over, taking his time about it. This operation had to go softly, very softly. Presently he said, "Not a damn thing, cowboy. Where's Dolly?"

The grin was beginning to look a bit strained as the guy replied, "She's inside. What's up?"

"Nothing's up," Bolan told him. He took the guy by the arm and moved him along toward the house.

"We heard about Dandy Jack," said the cowboy, still trying to cozy up. "That's a hell of a thing, isn't it?"

Bolan said, "Yeah. S'why I'm here. Relax. You're trying too hard."

"I'm not—uh—okay." The guy was getting nervous as hell; that much was obvious. "You said an errand for Mr. Copa. What uh . . . ?"

"I told you to relax. I came for Leonetti's woman and that's all I came for."

Relief was flooding that drawling voice as the guy responded to the news. "Oh, right, I knew—I told Dolly that would be the next move, the only logical next move. I mean, shit,

61

you gotta go with what you have." He was fitting a key to the lock as he spoke. The door swung open and the guy ushered Bolan inside with a flourish. "We all feel sorry for ol' Dandy but . . ."

Bolan growled, "Yeah," and went in.

Nothing in there was crumbling. A large entry foyer, lavish and ornate with marble statuary and red velvets led the way to a magnificently arched doorway and a huge room which may have originally been meant for formal balls. Now it seemed to be serving the function of sensuous reception, very artfully decorated and furnished with extravagance. A pair of broad curving staircases rose to a large balcony and more extravagance.

A pretty woman of about thirty came forward to greet the visitor. The joint would have been incomplete without her. The luxuriously buxom body was appealingly showcased in transparent lounging pajamas and nothing else. The hair was red—though probably not naturally so—soft and bouncy and framing an entirely comely face. But it was the face of a woman who had been everywhere, seen everything, and found the whole experience something less than lovely.

Bolan felt an inner tug of sympathy for that face.

The cowboy performed the introduction. "Dolly, this is Mr. Lambretta. He came to pick up your Russian."

"Why?" she said, looking directly at Bolan and not acknowledging the introduction.

"I didn't ask," Bolan replied coldly, returning the direct stare.

"Maybe I should," the woman said.

"That's for you to say. But do it quick. He doesn't like to wait."

"I know," she said quietly. Those hard eyes flashed with an acknowledgment of some inner truth. "Okay. Can't say I'm sorry to see her go. Nothing but a pain in the butt for me. Doesn't speak a damn word of English. Keeps the other girls torn up all the time. I've had to start sedating her. You'll have to carry her out. And you tell Mr. Copa I'd rather he didn't send her back here when he's finished with her."

"He can't do that, Dolly," said the cowboy in a hushed and scandalized voice. He shot Bolan an apologizing look as he said to him, "I'll give you a hand."

They went up the stairs in silence, the woman following slowly.

Smiley was in a garret room at the top of the house. Another girl shared the small room with her, a waif of perhaps sixteen with luminous eyes and a very frightened face. Smiley was conscious, but barely so. She wore only a flimsy, soiled shorty nightgown. There was no apparent recognition of the man bending over her and she made no protest as he gingerly examined her.

"Sedated, hell," Bolan growled. "You've got her bombed out of her mind. It'll take hours to bring her around."

The waif in the other bed raised to both elbows and said, in a quavery voice, "She's really okay. She started eating again last night. And I took her to the bathroom a little while ago. She's—"

"Shut up, Donna!" said the headwoman, harshly.

The girl rapidly batted those great eyes then closed them, lay back down, and turned her back on it all.

Bolan growled, "Get her clothes. Get some for Donna, too. She's coming with us."

"Now wait a minute," Dolly said.

"Do it, damnit!"

"Donna is still in the training program. It's too soon to—"

Boland roared, "What are you—deaf? I said do it!"

The kid came off the bed with a leap. "It's okay, Dolly," she urged breathlessly. "It's a good idea. I can handle her. I've been taking—"

"Sure it's okay," the cowboy said quickly. He was nervously moving the woman toward the door. "Go get the clothes. Mr. Lambretta knows what he's doing."

Indeed he did.

Minutes later, Mr. Lambretta's car was moving smoothly toward the gate with a pair of repatriated females in the back seat. He stopped at the gate to wedge a pebble into the locking mechanism, then went quickly on.

He caught the girl's frightened eyes in the rearview mirror and his voice was soft and warm as he asked her, "You okay, kid?"

"Yes sir, I'm fine," she assured him.

"Get ready for a surprise," he said. "This is

64

not at all what you probably think it is. You're going to be with some nice people. Cooperate with them, help them all you can. Okay?"

"Okay," the girl replied faintly.

Smiley was totally out of it, the tousled head resting on the girl's shoulder.

Two blocks from the school, Bolan turned into another drive where an ambulance and several other vehicles waited. Toby Ranger and Tommy Anders, showing anxious faces, moved quickly forward to receive their lost one.

"She's fine," Bolan assured them. "A bit wobbly now, but I think she'll be all right."

Toby had gone immediately to the rear seat. Anders halted at Bolan's window and reached in with a warm hand. "No sign of Carl?" he inquired.

"Not yet. Do you have your portable judge?"

"We have him. We also have your man Oxley appropriately iced."

"Keep him there," Bolan said grimly. "The others, too. Smiley's bombed out but the youngster here will give you what you need for the judge. I want you to hit them quick. Let's cover this one good."

"You know we will," the comic replied quietly.

Yeah. Bolan knew that they would. It was an efficient strike team. They would be all over that school before the inmates knew what was going down. And with all the rules of evidence meticulously honored. The charges would be kidnapping, white slavery, transport of females and minors across state lines for immoral purposes, and probably a half-dozen other major felonies. Even so, Bolan knew. . . .

"No bail, Tom," he muttered. "We can't have these people on the street for a while. We don't even want them communicating."

The little guy grinned sourly. "You can't bail 'til you're booked. Never fear. We'll keep them iced for at least twenty-four hours."

"It's a hell of a note," Bolan growled.

"Yeah. But it's the only note we got."

"It's the only note *you've* got," Bolan said, the eyes flashing.

"You aren't comfortable with our game, are you?"

"Not a bit," the big blitzer admitted.

The ambulance attendants were quickly taking Smiley away. Anders took a greatly confused teenage girl in tow. Toby Ranger paused at Bolan's window for a quick kiss and a misty-eyed thanks.

"It's going to be okay," she whispered.

"Be good to the kid," Bolan said gruffly. "She's had a rough time. Probably a runaway. Handle her gently, Toby."

He backed his vehicle out of there and went quickly on his way.

Time was becoming the all important factor, now.

And he only wished that he could share Toby's optimism. As a matter of fact, he did not. The "soft" was over. All that lay ahead was *hard*—double damn hard.

# CHAPTER 8

# QUESTION OF RIGHTS

Carl Lyons and Smiley Dublin, posing as Mr. and Mrs. Carl Leonetti, had made connections in the Orient with Dandy Jack Clemenza, a very ambitious minor echelon *Mafioso* who hoped to become the heroin king of North America. Clemenza had been making a pitch to the collective families of Mafia with assurances that he could, with their backing, corner the American import market in illegal drugs—and that, moreover, they could completely dominate the distribution and sale of the valuable substances within the United States.

Basically, that was the package on which Lyons and Dublin had been working. But the total picture was quite a bit larger than that—and it was the total picture which had been giving so much anguish to their partners, Tom Anders and Toby Ranger.

While Lyons and Dublin worked their wiles on the international scene, Anders and Ranger had thrown their total energy into the domestic side of the conspiracy with an attempt to draw straight lines of cause and effect relationships which would eventually ensnare and topple the whole large network of organized crime in America. Just as, in earlier times, the feds had used income tax evasion as an effective inroad to the heavily insulated higher ranks, they now hoped to ride the narcotics trails into those ranks—though with much more devastating results.

The entire set of jinks via Lyons and Dublin was intended to interface with that higher purpose. So much had been made in recent years of constitutional guarantees to criminals—especially with respect to the concepts of entrapment and illegally obtained evidence—that the professional criminals had been laughing up their sleeves and enjoying a free ride on this noble ideal of freemen while systematically plundering the rights and properties of those same men. It seemed to Bolan that very often the nobler thinkers of society tried to regard rights as some esthetic essence quite unrelated to the real world. The whole business of crime and punishment had thus become ritualized as some weirdly formal game between the good guys and the bad—with that distinction often blurred in the interplay of rights versus justice—and with never a thought to the real-world rights of society itself.

Bolan knew a thing or two about real world rights.

These involved the right of any good citizen to walk his streets without fear, to be free from intimidation and illegal exploitation, free from degradation and bodily harm and violence in all its guises—primarily, though, the right to work and save and build and keep.

There was no right to plunder.

Yet the noble thinkers seemed to believe that there was unless the rituals of the game were rigidly honored.

Mack Bolan lived in the real world. He therefore did not subscribe to such unworldly beliefs. Lawmen lived in the real world, also, and were forced to subscribe—if they were to be allowed into the game at all. Thus, the fantastic intrigues such as the present situation, the incredible personal risks, the often tragic consequences.

The SOG attempted a penetration of a highly organized and well layered outfit. The players within this outfit knew the game well and had mastered all the rituals. The game was also, as always, heavily rigged in their favor since the lawmen were the only players who were required to observe any rules whatever. The penetration—obviously so successful in the base phase—had just as obviously fallen apart between the layers. Lyons had served as Clemenza's personal courier by accompanying the heroin shipment from the Far East to an intermediate point in South America. Another courier had taken over at that point, moving the junk into the Central American corridor and eventually into the U.S.

According to the game plan, then, Lyons was to have returned to his Far East headquarters upon completion of the base leg. Instead, and according to a higher game plan, he had come on to Nashville in an attempt to bridge the layers and establish a meaningful rapport with the domestic distributors. Apparently he had failed in that attempt. And very probably, yeah, the consequences of that failure were tragic.

Bolan held little hope that he would find Carl Lyons, alias Leonetti, alive and well.

Meanwhile the game had gone on. The plays had already been called and there was nothing to be gained by calling an audible at the line of scrimmage. Anders and Ranger went on with their part in the intrigue, hoping against all odds that somehow the play could yet be saved, well aware that sometimes it is the busted play that brings the largest gain.

As a final, forlorn gamble, Bolan had been called in at the last moment to lend his own brand of razzle-dazzle broken field running to the problem. In any clear analysis, sure, that represented a violation of the ritual. But there was a hell of a lot more at stake here than some esthetic appreciation of constitutional rights and governmental restraints. These were real people inhabiting a real world—and the most vicious section of it at that. And Bolan understood their despair. He shared it. And though he had agreed to walk softly in this hallowed game of rituals and rights, he knew that he had used all the soft at his disposal.

It was, yes, a well layered organization. And Ray Oxley had been accurate in at least one important respect: it was an outfit which did not appear to follow traditional Mafia patterns. That was another negative for Bolan. He was working largely in the dark on this one, going on instincts as much as anything else as he sought the keys to this patchwork outfit. At this layer, it seemed to be composed mostly of minor minions of the organized crimeworld—guys who had always seemed content to operate relatively independent little territories at the very edge of Mafia power, primarily in quasi-legitimate business areas.

Roxy Artists was typical of the breed. Despite Oxley's protestations to the contrary, he actually was an owner. He owned 23 percent of Roxy. But that was his sole interest in the larger network which included recording companies, booking agencies, theaters, clubs, hotels and casinos through the Western Hemisphere.

Moreover, Bolan was sure that patient probing would also uncover an invisible network of allied companies in such areas as real estate development and management, laundries, vending machines, janitorial services, and various other services and suppliers—such as the Juliana Academy and its rotten little approach to liberal lifestyling.

It was a disturbingly familiar game. Only the players, at the visible level, supplied the difference. But it was a difference which spelled *insurance* for the other levels and *great difficulty* for those hoping to penetrate beyond the visible, even though Bolan was practically certain that the same old familiar faces would be found hovering in the invisible background and pulling the strings.

And he was beginning to appreciate the full scope of the Justice Department's interest in all this. No matter how legitimate a Mafia operation might appear on the surface, the Mafia mentality simply did not allow room for any business approach which was not inherently rapacious and destructive to its environment.

Roxy Artists would serve as a case in point. Since the same invisible interests controlled both the agency and the various showplaces—including even recording companies and distributors, perhaps even radio stations—any promising young talent falling into Roxy's clutches was a tailormade mark for the game of rape and loot. The kid would be fully exploited from every possible angle while sharing very little of the profits, squeezed dry, then flung back into the dust to make room for another. Some of the unfortunate ones would no doubt be turned out for prostitution (whether male or female), doping, organized thievery, con games, or whatever. As always, wherever encountered and at whatever level, a Mafia presence was a societal cancer.

In this particular instance, the tip of the iceberg represented by Oxley and his Roxy Artists was a monstrous growth which threatened to undermine the entire social structure built up around the entertainment industry.

And, no, Bolan was not feeling particularly concerned over the legal rights of the plunderers.

Until Nashville, he had been only minimally aware of the existence of the hood called Nick Copa—also known variously as Cupaletto, Copaletta, Cupaletti, and Copoletto. He was a cousin to the late Anthony "Tony Danger" Cupaletto, a Californian. Copa was now about forty-two years of age and had no criminal record, although it was known that his early years had been spent as a feared enforcer for the DiGeorge Family of southern California. The federal government's crimewatch had carried no mention of Copa, or whoever, until very recently and even that mention was followed by a question mark.

On the other hand, Gordon "Crazy Gordy" Mazzarelli was quite well known to federal watchers. Though the thirty-five-year-old professional gunman had never been convicted of a felony, the arrest record was quite extensive and covered a period of thirteen years—most of it involving viciously violent crimes. He was regarded in the underworld as a sadistic and conscienceless enforcer for the Mafia masters, and he was generally given a wide berth by all who knew his reputation.

Mazzarelli had been a resident of Tennessee for only a few months, apparently arriving on the scene at about the same time that Copa first became visible in the area. There was no record of prior association between the two. Copa was a Californian whereas Mazzarelli was a native of East Chicago and had apparently confined his operations to the Midwest until very recently.

So the patchwork effect was evident at this level of the outfit, as well. And this was indeed a bother to the methodical mind of Mack Bolan. Something new seemed to be arising from the patchwork, and it was something quite larger and far more elaborate than a mere distribution network for narcotics.

Perhaps Bolan himself was indirectly responsible for this new look in Mafia organization. The whole national pattern had fallen out of focus with his shatteringly successful command strike against the national headquarters in New York, several campaigns back. So maybe the Nashville Look was an inevitable consequence of the leadership vacuum at the national level.

The Executioner intended to get a closer look.

He would give the soft approach one more go. Not because of any personal regard for the constitutional rights of the players—they had relinquished those rights when they entered the game—but because of his great personal respect for the other side. The SOGs had a considerable investment in this exercise in terms of time, energy, and perhaps life itself. Bolan had no wish to trample on that investment.

So—he would try the soft game once more. But he was not losing sight of the fact that *this* was a *war* and that *they* were the *enemy*. And if soft walking produced nothing more satisfying than the *bones* of Carl Lyons then it was going to quickly become a damned *hard* war, indeed.

Assuming, of course, that Bolan could survive one more soft walk.

There were no *rights* to guarantee such an outcome—except, maybe, the rights vested by jungle law—and, of course, Mack Bolan understood that law very well.

# CHAPTER 9

# ACES FULL

The little bubblefront helicopter lifted off with a rush and began climbing over the city on a southeasterly course. "It's just a few minutes away," Grimaldi warned his passenger.

Bolan nodded his head in silent response and continued his preparations. Already the river was far behind them, the downtown area quickly giving way to the gently rolling suburban terrain. This was bluegrass country, sort of poised between the high mountains to the east and the Mississippi River delta lands to the west. Geographers referred to the middle Tennessee country as the Highland Rim. Residents simply called it God's Country—and Bolan had to agree with them. But a particular patch of it was soon to become hellgrounds, and there was no way to avoid that determination.

He completed the cosmetic job on his hair. It was jet black once again and quite a bit more conservatively styled. The Beretta Belle was in a snapaway shoulder rig, nestling inconspicuously beneath expensive threads.

"How does it look?" he asked his friend, the Mafia pilot.

"Looks like you invented them, guy," the pilot muttered.

Grimaldi did not like this operation. He had tried his best to talk Bolan out of it.

"Then I guess I'm ready when you are, Jack."

Grimaldi turned a searching look on his friend as he replied to that. "You'd better be *damned* ready. Like I said, it wasn't much of a recon. But *trouble* screamed up at me from every corner of that joint. I counted six vehicles in the main parking area. There's room for another four in garages. The helicopter pad is about fifty yards from the rear of the main house. From the air it looks like it's had plenty of use. And those damn barns . . . listen, I didn't see a head of stock anywhere. No horses, no cows, nothing. But things are happening inside those outbuildings. Lots of activity. Guys all over the place, very busy. And I could smell it from a thousand feet up. It's a hotspot, buddy. So you watch your ass in there."

"Thanks, I'll do that," Bolan replied drily.

Yeah. He would do that. He would have preferred a first hand look before settling into that joint. But time was in the saddle, riding every consideration of the day. So he'd been forced to settle for a quick flyover by Grimaldi while the Juliana Academy thing was going down. And the pilot had liked not a damn thing he'd seen there. How much more dislike would a trained scout have found at Nick Copa's highland hideaway?

Bolan shook the question away and focused his mind on the positive aspects. There were one or two of those, sure.

"There it is, soldier," Grimaldi said suddenly. "Three o'clock horizon."

So there it was. A line of buildings nestled atop a wooded ridge, pastures flowing to lower elevations at either side and serving as buffer zones, lots of fencing to augment the natural barriers.

Hellgrounds, yeah.

The pilot sighed. "Last chance to change your mind."

"Go straight in," Bolan instructed. "Set down on the pad. I go out, you go up. Just like that."

"And I come back in an hour," Grimaldi growled.

"Precisely one hour. But you don't land unless you get a beep."

"Suppose your radio is not working?"

"Then neither am I," Bolan replied in a matter-of-fact tone. "No beep, no landing. You return to Nashville. And call off the play."

"What do I tell them?"

"Tell them the side's retired. One hit, no runs, one man left on."

"That's a hell of a way to put it. So then what do I do?"

"Then you go home, Jack. With my blessings."

"Bullshit, I don't like it."

"Neither do I. What's that have to do with anything?"

"They're liable to hit you even if they buy you. Think of that?"

"Thanks, I've been trying not to."

"We can still scrub."

"It's not a scrub. It's a go. So let's go."

They went. Grimaldi flew a beeline in gradual descent and put her down on the little raised area of rear lawn. Not a head was showing anywhere back there.

"Go get 'em, tiger," the pilot said tautly.

Bolan gripped the firm hand as he muttered, "Way to go," and stepped to the ground.

The chopper lifted away as soon as he moved into the clear.

The lawn was thick, luxurious, well tended. Tennis court, left—fancy aquatic gardens, right. The sprawling ranchstyle house was ultramodern with plenty of glass and stone— huge, elegant.

Hellgrounds for sure, though.

Bolan produced a slim gold case from a breast pocket and extracted a long brown cigarillo as he casually studied the layout. He could feel the invisible force of eyes upon him. But no one was showing himself. He lit the cigarillo and wandered across the lawn toward the house.

And he knew exactly how Daniel had felt, in the den of lions.

The big man who stepped from the helicopter had *headshed* etched into him. It wasn't just the handtailored threads and flashy good looks but something more subtle, some quiet essence that whispered power instead of yelling it, an aura of self confidence and absolute control.

"Wonder what he wants," Copa murmured as he handed the glasses to his head cock.

"Recognize him?" Mazzarelli asked as he raised the binoculars to his eyes.

"Only the type. You?"

"Never seen 'im," the head cock decided, after a long scrutiny. "Not with *that* face, anyway. But you're right. That's what he is. What nerve. I hear it's open season on those guys."

"Not officially," Copa said. "Not yet, anyway." He took back the glasses and again trained them on the visitor. "Like to try him?"

Mazzarelli chuckled coldly. "Not without good reason. I got no beef with those guys. Never hurt me none."

"Then maybe you'd better make him feel welcome." Copa lowered the glasses and sighed, the face settling into lines of displeasure. "Wonder what the hell he *wants*."

"A free meal, maybe," said Mazzarelli. He took a small radio from a waist clip and passed a guarded all-clear to his troops. "Bring him in, boys. And handle with care."

Copa watched the reception then turned away from the window and pressed a button on the desk intercom. An instant response came from the house cock.

"Yeah, boss?"

"You heard the chopper, Lenny. Looks like we got company from New York. One guy. Set up the garden patio. Let's make it, uh, *Tia Maria* and something light, just some munchies—you know. Uh, let's put a couple of the hottest pretties in the pool. Tell them to look stunning and keep quiet. And tell Mrs. Copa she'll join us in ten minutes. That is exactly ten minutes from right now. Hop to it."

One of Mazzarelli's boys was at the door of the study a moment later. He wordlessly passed through a small leather ID wallet. Mazzarelli took a quick look and tossed it on to his boss. "You were right," he commented sourly. "You ever see one of those before?"

"What is it?" Copa asked, instead of looking at the ID.

"It's a Black Ace. Funny. All these years and it's the first I seen."

"Don't feel bad about *that*," Copa muttered. He opened the wallet and peered at the elegantly embossed and plasticized playing card encased there. "Ace of *Spades*, Gordy. It's a *death* card."

"Wonder what the hell he wants here."

"So do I."

"Maybe you better call."

"Damn right I'm going to call," Copa replied anxiously. He produced a ring of keys and fitted one into a large drawer of the desk, opened the drawer, and lifted out a "funny phone" which he set delicately down on the desk.

Mazzarelli growled, "You want me to go out and—?"

"No, not yet. Let's confirm this hot ass first."

The Boss of Nashville donned reading glasses and consulted a small notebook which he withdrew from the base of the telephone. Then he lifted the phone and punched up a long combination on the relay diffuser. Thirty seconds later he had his roundabout connection into New York—via Atlanta, Dallas, Denver and Boston.

The greeting had the metallic resonance which he had come to associate with the scrambler lines. *"Headshed."*

"Area Three here," he responded. "I need a playing card confirmation."

*"Hold it."*

Another instrument clicked into the line almost instantly and a different voice announced, *"Field Bureau."*

"Yeah. Area Three, here. This is Highroller. I want a make on a black card."

*"What's the number, sir?"*

"Who am I talking to?"

*"This is Auditor, sir."*

"Okay. This is in Spades. It's zero two, dash, zero two, dash, one one one."

*"That's a Full House, sir. I can't give you that. I'll have to pass you higher."*

"Do it, then, damnit, and snap it up. I got the man waiting."

*"One moment, please."*

Copa covered the transmitter with his fingers and asked his head cock, "What's a Full House?"

"You mean . . . ?" Mazzarelli's gaze flicked toward the door. "Beats me. Sounds like a high hand, though."

"Right." Copa fidgeted and shook the telephone angrily, muttering, "Goddamn bureaucratic bullshit. I never saw such—you better take the man to the garden, Gordy. But watch him. Treat him with respect, but watch him. It may take awhile to check this out."

Mazzarelli nodded his understanding and went quickly out to greet the visitor.

Copa waited and fumed at the silent telephone, staring at the "calling card" until his eyes glazed with the effort. At this particular time, an Ace of Spades was bad enough. A Full House sounded even more ominous—and he wanted none of it whatever it meant.

Mazzarelli was right, though. The *commissione's* Aces had fallen onto hard times. They had been all but repudiated by the surviving council of bosses, following the unbelievable fiasco in New York which had crumbled the Marinello empire. Now these hotasses were under tight leashes from their headshed and it was being told around that many of them dared not venture away from the New York area. A lot of wiseguys around the world were holding hot bags of hate for the former untouchables. Several of them had been hit in recent weeks, or so the stories went.

Like Mazzarelli, Nick Copa had no particular reason to dislike the Aces. The guys had done a hell of a job during a damn tough period. They'd kept the families from slaughtering one another, and they'd brought a stability to an organization which by its very nature was patently unstable. Copa gave them all due credit for that. And he had no reason to hate them.

He also, however, had no particular reason not to hit them—if any got in his way.

And that went for Full Houses, too.

# CHAPTER 10

# NUANCES

It was a strange world, this world of Mafia. As with most secret societies, it was held together by a rather rigid social structure and governed by quiet ritual. Custom and tradition were therefore important elements and tended to persist long beyond practical usage. It was this understanding of Mafia mind in which Bolan was investing his own strange game. He knew that the Aces had become an endangered species —thanks chiefly to his own destructive penetration of their ranks. They had constituted an elite force—a secret society within the secret society—with virtually unlimited power and authority in the internal affairs of the Mafia nation. They had been, in effect, a sort of *gestapo*. And it was a tailormade setup for a guy like Mack Bolan.

He had been walking quietly among them

since the third campaign of his war against the Mafia, taking on their camouflage when the "need versus risk" factor seemed to be in balance. It was not, however, a masquerade which a guy would contemplate for extended periods, or for capricious purposes. His enemies were not fools, even though he frequently made them appear as such. Bolan had survived this far in his war not by contempt for his enemy, but by careful respect for their intelligence and cunning. Each penetration was always on the heartbeat, with Bolan's survival in their midst directly dependent upon every word being spoken to the finest nuance, each gesture carried to perfection, every movement of face and eyes geared to the dictates of the changing moment.

It was not a fun thing, not even under the best of circumstances.

Add to that the present reality that Bolan's recent command strike on New York had severely undermined the authority of the gestapo force. In the immediate wake of that strike it had seemed highly improbable that the superhard force would survive at all. But it was a strange world and the Aces had survived, although in greatly modified form. They were no longer autonomous. They could not interfere in any intrafamily dispute and their function in the no man's land between families was purely as fact-finders and arbitrators. Theoretically they were still at the disposal for hard duties—of that council of bosses known as *La Commissione*. So they were, in theory, still an enforcement arm of that council. But the council itself was presently in disarray, due to the instability of the Mafia world itself. It had not formally met since the New York fiasco, and *La Commissione* was in fact nothing more now than an executive staff functioning almost entirely as an administrative service. They maintained communications, and coordinated various operations between the underworld groups.

All of this left the Aces as neither fish nor fowl in that predatory jungle constituting the Mafia world. A few had been hit—as the logical settlement (in this world) of old grievances. Others had simply drifted away and vanished, retiring, perhaps, to obscure fates. Those that remained in service did so at their constant peril—at least until a new stability could be established.

So Bolan was well aware of the various hazards involved in this attempt to softly penetrate the Copa camp. But he was banking on that strange quality of Mafia mind which finds its sustenance in tradition, custom, and ritual. And he knew that success could be measured only from one heartbeat to the next.

He was not here for fun and games.

Mazzarelli was a bear of a man, half a head shorter than Bolan but commanding 300 pounds or more of tightly packed brawn— shoulders a yard wide, neck and head appearing as one unit with hardly any variation in circumference. The face was something else, though. Except for the bristly crewcut hair, it recalled memories of the long-dead comedian

Lou Costello—radiating that same air of tragi-comic innocence and vulnerability. But Bolan knew better. This guy was as dangerous as a riled rattlesnake. All the time.

"Call me Omega," Bolan told him. He did not offer his hand.

"Okay, call me Gordy," said the Bear. The name fit no better than the face. The smile was pure *mama mia* and could have been entirely disarming had Bolan not known what lurked behind the smile. "How're things in the Big Apple?"

"Tense," Bolan replied.

"I'll bet, yeah. I haven't been there in a long time. I hate that damn town."

"That's okay," said Bolan-Omega. "I hate Chicago."

Those "innocent" eyes buckled a bit. "You like Nashville?"

"Better than Chicago, yeah."

"I'm from *East* Chicago, you know."

Bolan knew, sure. And he knew this word game, too. "I hate it worse," he said pleasantly.

It was a tense little verbal shoving match, a jockeying for status. Every kid who'd ever been on a schoolyard would recognize this game.

Mazzarelli said, "Yeah?"

Bolan replied, "Yeah. How 'bout you?"

The guy retreated with a chuckle. "Right, right. That's why I come south. Guess I could stay here the rest of my life."

Bolan would try to see to that. He said, "Nick's checking me out, eh?"

"Sure. Wouldn't you?"

90

According to the rules of the game, it was now Bolan's turn to retreat—if, that is, he wished to demonstrate style. He chuckled as he replied. "I hope he doesn't get a wild man up there with a sick sense of humor."

It was enough; not too much. Mazzarelli understood the finer naunces of the word game. The smile became genuine as he stuck out a hamlike paw. Bolan shook the hand and smiled back. The Bear said, "Glad you could make it. We're setting up hospitality in the garden. It's very nice out there. You'll like it. Nick wants you should get comfortable and feel at home. Can you stay awhile?"

Bolan made it sound like a regret. "Not long, no."

They crossed a large room featuring a vaulted ceiling and two outer walls of glass. Directly beyond was an elevated garden overlooking the pool. Pools, rather. One was for swimming; numerous others very obviously were not—they were ponds, actually, containing varieties of aquatic plants and clustered about the large central pool to create a beautifully tropic effect. Exotic potted plants and miniature trees combined with all that for a stunningly sensual experience. Swimming there, one would have the definite sensation of a paradise.

Two beautiful girls in microscopic bikinis added a positive dimension to that effect.

"Nice, huh," Mazzarelli said proudly.

Bolan laughed lightly and said, "Maybe I *could* stay awhile."

"Stay as long as you like," said the Bear. "Summer, winter—it's all the same here."

Bolan could believe that. The whole garden area was enclosed within a dome-like metallic framework in which were emplaced hinged panels of tinted glass. Apparently the panels could be opened or closed for changing environmental needs.

"I'd get soft, here," Bolan growled appreciatively.

Mazzarelli laughed. "No way," he said. "Not with Nick around. And speak of the devil . . ."

The lord of the manse was approaching, making his appearance via another doorway into the garden. He was a handsome man of medium size and graceful carriage. The sight of him triggered a small peephole in Bolan's mental mugfile, bringing to mind the memory of a long obscure intelligence file on the guy. And Bolan had him made, now. Years ago, they had called him "the Professor" because of his interest in books. It was said that he nursed ambitions to be an author and had once been severely reprimanded for maintaining a clandestine diary toward a future attempt at autobiography. All that had been years ago, while he served the late Mafia lord of Los Angeles, Julian "Deej" DiGeorge. There was very little open knowledge of Copa's activities during recent years.

He came forward, hand outstretched, and smiling broadly. "Omega . . . it's a pleasure, a sincere pleasure."

Bolan shook hands and they sat down at a

small table in a grove of miniature palms. The pool was directly ahead and about ten feet below. The bathing beauties were splashing quietly and without much animation in the shallow end. Bolan recognized them for what they were—stage props—as much a part of the scenery as the potted plants surrounding them. A couple of hard-looking guys in white coats were ceremoniously attending to the refreshments which had been wheeled up in elegant serving carts.

Meanwhile, it was small talk time.

Mazzarelli said, "Omega says he'd get soft here, Nick. I can't believe that. Can you?"

The boss of Nashville laughed politely as he replied, "He's pulling your leg, Gordy. Omega here is the hardest case New York can send. So you better get worried. He didn't come all the way down here to romp in the Garden of Eden."

"No I didn't," Bolan admitted, smiling. "But I'm almost converted. This must have cost a lot of bucks, Nick."

Copa the *capo* waved his hand in dismissal of the consideration as he replied, "What's money for if not to improve the quality of life? I've got a hundred and sixty acres here of God's country. It's my own little kingdom. Everything I need and want is right here. How do you put a price tag on that?"

Bolan said, "You're right."

Mazzarelli had not come that far in the conversation. He quietly asked, "What should I be worried about?"

Copa arched an eyebrow at Bolan and laughed softly. "What should he be worried about, Omega?"

Bolan did not laugh with him. The small talk was ended. Very softly, he replied, "Plenty." The nuance was perfect.

And the Bear did not like it. He was very obviously on the defensive as he asked. "Did this guy check out, Nick?"

"Of course he checked out." Copa made a little ceremony of returning the ID wallet to Bolan. "That," he said soberly, for Mazzarelli's benefit, "is an Aces' Full House. What Omega wants, Omega gets in this territory." The next was directed only at the visitor. "Let's talk like men."

Bolan nodded. "You always do, Nick."

The Professor liked that nuance. He said, "Thanks. Here's what I want to say. I don't know anything about the troubles in New York. I'm not part of them and they're not part of me. I have no complaints with the administration. You guys have been doing a whale of a job and my doors are wide open to you. If you have a problem then I have a problem and vice versa. Like I said, my doors are wide open. But I run a tight ship. I don't want you doing anything in my territory unless you've cleared it with me, first. Now that's about as plain as I can put it."

"That's plain enough," Bolan replied, not committing himself to anything further.

"So why are you here?"

"I came to get Carl Leonetti."

"Who?"

The Bolan gaze turned fully upon Mazzarelli although it was clear that he was responding to the other. "You'll remember Roberto. Carl is his kid."

Copa thought about that for a moment before quietly replying, "That goes way back. Roberto's wife and kid disappeared ten, fifteen years ago. You're not still looking for *them*?"

"The lady died ten years ago. The kid did not. He came to Nashville last week. He's needed in New York. I came to take him home."

Mazzarelli's eyes became noncommital slits, but the rest of the face was pure *mama mia* once again. "You mean you came to hit 'im," he said.

"I mean exactly what I said," Bolan told him.

"Wait a minute here," Copa said, in obvious confusion—and it seemed genuine. "There's more to this than I'm hearing. Why would Roberto's kid be in *my* territory? What's this all about?"

That was good enough for Bolan. It confirmed a feeling he'd had almost from the beginning. "Gordy can tell you more about that than I can," he said quietly.

The Copa gaze traveled quickly and compellingly to his lieutenant. "What's this all about?"

"I thought I told you," Mazzarelli said blandly.

"Told me what?"

"It's no big deal. I guess it wasn't important enough and I just forgot. Clemenza ran into the Leonetti kid awhile back when he was on a buying trip. You know. I think they had some kind of business deal. I don't know for sure. Anyway, Leonetti turns up here, maybe a week ago. In town, I mean. I guess he was looking for a connection."

"Did he say he was hot?"

"He didn't say, Nick."

"What *did* he say?"

Bolan was clearly no longer a participant in the conversation at the table. It was almost as though the other two had forgotten his presence. Which is perhaps why he was the first to become aware of the lady. He did not know how long she had been standing there in the background. But there she was—very striking, very lovely. She wore a silk lounging suit—on the order of a jumpsuit—and wore it very well. The dark hair was shoulder length and tawny, the eyes large and suffering. The age was anyone's guess but Bolan would call it quite a big younger than Copa. And there was something very familiar about that haunted, pretty face.

Bolan came to his feet and greeted her with, "Well, hello."

That ended the private conversation between the other two. Copa stood up quickly and took the lady's hand. He told Bolan-Omega, "I said everything I wanted was right here. This is most of it. Omega, meet Mrs. Copa. Maybe you already know her as Molly Franklin."

Of course. Most people in the country would have found something very familiar about the

96

lady. She was one of the current legends of the Nashville music scene. She'd come to this town as a raggedy teenager from a mountain hamlet with a suitcase full of original music and a voice to give unique life to that music. And she'd conquered Music City long ago, very nearly conquering all of America, as well, through television appearances in recent years.

Bolan murmured an acknowledgement of the introduction and the four sat down to small talk and light refreshments. After several minutes, Copa suggested that the lady show the visitor around the garden. She softly acquiesced. Bolan and the lady wandered away. Copa and Mazzarelli immediately returned to their original conversation.

She was showing Bolan a rubber tree which overhung the swimming pool, speaking almost mechanically in that soft drawl of the problems inherent in tropical gardening in Tennessee, when she shifted smoothly into another problem much closer to Mack Bolan's interests.

"Can you get me out of here?" she quietly inquired.

He was not certain that he heard her rightly. "What?"

"Can you get me *out* of here?"

"Can't you get yourself out?"

"I wouldn't be asking *you* if I could."

"Are you a prisoner?"

"Yes I am a prisoner. In my own home. This is *my* home, damnit! And he won't let me—will you take me with you?"

Bolan took her arm and moved her along the pool's edge. "What makes you think I can?"

"The whole house has been buzzing ever since you got here. I've heard nothing else. You're an important man. I know you can take me away if you want to."

"I wouldn't want to get in the middle of a family spat," he told her.

"It is *not* a family spat." She shot a look of pure hatred toward the table. "Let him have it. I just want *out* of here."

"Let him have what?"

"The house, the land, all of it. But not *me*. I want out."

All of which was very interesting and intriguing to Bolan the Bold . . . but perhaps also a complication which might prove very hazardous to the mission goal.

He told the lady, "You put me in a very delicate position."

The lady told the visitor. "Well you won't find what you're looking for here."

He said, "You know what I'm looking for?"

"I heard enough that I can guess. You won't find him here. Her, either. Get me out and I'll tell you where to find them."

Complicating, yeah. But very, very interesting. Unless the lady was merely grasping at straws.

"Convince me," Bolan said quietly.

"He's from Singapore. He has a Russian wife. Gordy is trying to—and we—the flowering plants make such a *mess* of the pool, and we . . ."

She'd shifted back just in time. Copa was moving toward them . . . almost upon them.

Bolan told the lady with the haunted face, "I'm convinced. You've got a real problem there."

Copa said, "No problem can't be fixed. Right, honey?"

"I don't know," she said coldly.

"Depends on the proper approach," Bolan said, speaking for the benefit of both. He made eye contact with the lady and put as much understanding as he could gather there. "You have to pick your own time and place. I always do that." He turned to her husband. "Right, Nick?"

Copa laughed and said, "Better listen to the man, honey. Troubleshooting is his business."

"I heard every word he said," the lady assured her husband.

Yeah. Bolan was sure of that.

She'd heard, also, every word he had not said.

So now what?

## CHAPTER 11

# TROUBLESHOOTING

They had been silently strolling the grounds and had reached a point about midway between the house and the outbuildings when Copa soberly declared, "I hope you don't mind me walking your legs off. I think better on my feet."

Indeed, Bolan did not mind the walk. He was getting a good feel of the place. And he was getting an even better feel of the man. "You're lucky to have a place like this, Nick," he told him. "The cities are just getting to be too much. New York has gone completely crazy. The others aren't far behind."

"Don't I know it," said the other. "Take L.A. Take Chicago. Take even Vegas. Artificial. It's all artificial." Several paces farther, the conversation turned to a serious note. "Omega, I'm worried."

"Uh huh. About Gordy?"

"Who else?"

"How long has he been with you now?" Bolan inquired.

"Just long enough for me to start wondering. I didn't know him very well, before. Just his reputation. You?"

Bolan grinned. "They didn't start calling him Crazy Gordy for nothing."

The responding grin was more of a grimace. "He's crazy all right. Like a fox."

Bolan was treading a delicate line. He kept that balance as he told the boss of Nashville, "I know nothing behind him, Nick. Far as we know, he's always been a good company man."

"Far as we *know*, right. But what is all this shit, Omega? What's going on?"

"What did Gordy tell you?"

"He said Roberto's kid came in from the Orient looking for a connection. Said he was worried about the old trouble and didn't know where he stood. Said he was quietly asking around. Gordy says he met with the kid, in town. Had dinner with him and his wife. They small talked. The kid asked for nothing, Gordy offered him nothing. They were supposed to meet again, the next day. The kid was going to call to confirm the meet. He didn't call. Gordy says that's all he knows."

"Maybe that's straight and maybe it's not," Bolan-Omega said quietly. "There's more here than meets the eye."

"So I figured, yeah. But why would he lie about it?"

102

"That's for you to say," Bolan replied cryptically. "But I have to tell you, Nick . . . the reason I came down . . ."

"Don't stop there. Say it."

"Well, you've got a problem here."

"Don't I know it. I guess you know that Dandy Jack took a big fall last night. This is tied to that, somehow, isn't it?"

Bolan said, "I'm afraid it is, Nick."

"Gordy and this Leonetti kid. They're part of that."

"Right. Only the kid is no longer a kid. He's a man. With ideas. You know."

Copa knew, sure. "I see."

"He was Clemenza's man in the Far East."

"Is that a fact?"

"It's a fact, Nick."

The guy had a great poker face. "I see."

"Here's the way we get it."

"I'm listening," said the Lord of Nashville. He was paying no attention whatever to the direction of their stroll. Bolan was deftly maneuvering the course toward the large central barn.

"Leonetti brought in the shipment that went down with Clemenza last night. He—"

"But the goods arrived just yesterday. The kid hit town—"

"He was supposed to have dropped it off in South America. And he did. But he did not return to home base, like he was supposed to. Instead, he hopped a plane to Nashville. Not to Memphis, Nick. To Nashville."

"I see. Why?"

"The way we make it, he was carrying another shipment."

A moment later, Copa said, "I see."

Damn right he saw.

So did Bolan. They were directly opposite the barn, now. The huge sliding doors were partially agape. A row of large packing crates were stacked just inside. The floor was slick and clean. But it was still too far away to give up any secrets.

The Mafia boss was deep in thought, his mind far removed from the stretch of turf at his feet.

"What, uh—this, uh—are you saying that Clemenza's fall last night is related to all this? Directly, I mean?"

"All I'm saying," Bolan quietly replied, "is that Dandy Jack had a secret competitor. Let's call him X. So X hits the scene about a week before Dandy's stuff is scheduled to arrive. Very conveniently, for X, Dandy then takes a fall—all his product with him. Which leaves X in a very fortunate position. Wouldn't you say?"

"I'd say, yeah," Copa growled softly. "And where does that put Z?"

Meaning, of course, Mazzarelli.

Bolan said, "Depends on where he stands with X, I'd say."

"So would I," said the boss. "How sure are you of all of this?"

"Sure enough that I came as quick as I could," said the visiting Ace.

"I appreciate that. Okay. So I've got a problem. Thanks."

Bolan said, "More than maybe it seems right off, Nick. We, uh—it's so delicate, we, uh—we didn't want to barge in."

"No, no, it's okay," the boss assured the visitor. "I appreciate it."

Bolan could now read the lettering on the crates in the barn. Electronic equipment.

"Who, uh—I have to ask—who funded the buy?"

"Oh, well—you know—a lot of people are in this. Who's funding Leonetti?"

"The same people," Bolan replied.

"I don't, uh, get your meaning," Copa said slowly.

"It's a shell game."

"Who's got the shells?"

"X has one of them, for sure. Z has one, maybe."

"I still don't get you."

"Can we talk straight out, Nick?"

"Like men, right. Go ahead."

"How much was invested in the product you lost last night?"

"Cash outlay, over a million. Street value—hell, it's—"

"Forget the street value. Let's talk cash from the pocket. You say over a million. What if I suggest to you that what you lost last night in Memphis was worth about half that?"

"Is that what you're saying?"

"I'm saying *what if*. What if our boy Leonetti got an exceptionally good price in Singapore. What if he was able to actually *double* the value of the buy? And what if he saw a way to sell you your own goods twice?"

Copa was now chewing invisible nails. "Go on."

Nobody hates to be suckered more than a guy who makes his living suckering others. The bare possibility was eating at Copa's guts.

Bolan quickly sank the spurs a bit deeper. "I believe that Leonetti was really trying to contact *you*, Nick. But he didn't get there."

"He runs into someone else first," Copa said thickly, picking it up for himself.

"That's what I'm saying, Nick. And this Leonetti kid has not been seen since."

The guy's anger was strangling him. "Okay, thanks," he grunted. "I'll handle it. Thanks for ..."

Bolan put a hand on the guy's arm and said, "First things first, Nick. You'll want to safe the investment. Right?"

"Naturally."

"You can still pull it out. That's all I'm suggesting. Leonetti is either at the bottom of the river or he's still around somewhere, under wraps. Either way, the product is here. In your territory. You've already paid for it. It's yours. Right?"

Copa was getting the anger under control. He said, "Go on. Say what you're saying, damnit."

"Don't tip your hand to Gordy. Tip *mine*."

"Meaning what?"

"Drop it on him that I'm really looking for a secret shipment that came in with X. Tell him

I almost have it wrapped. I checked in with you just for the courtesy."

Bolan wondered if he had pushed too hard. Copa was stiffening, mentally resisting. The response was troubled, thoughtful. "I never liked cat and mouse, Omega."

So Bolan pulled back. "Forget it, then. It's your territory and your problem. I just wanted you to know."

"I appreciate it, sure," said the boss. "You came a long way—I appreciate it."

They were now less than twenty paces from the barn. A hard looking guy stepped through the opening between the hanging doors, a submachine gun cradled at his chest. Bolan's mental mugfile clicked to an immediate make. It was one Rudi Folani, an old pro who'd last been noted in the St. Louis area.

Bolan said to Copa, "God, you've dredged them from everywhere, haven't you?"

Copa growled, "I like to stick with the tried and true. But maybe it's not always such a good idea."

They were ten paces out when Bolan called ahead, "How's it swinging, Rudi?"

The guy did a doubletake as he replied, "There's still a few swings left in it, sir. Do I know you, sir?"

Bolan winked at Copa as he replied, "You'd better not."

Folani understood the meaning of that. It was an embarrassment, a breach of ritual. "Right, sir, I'm sorry."

Copa was still engaged in the inner struggle

with his own troubles, but he seemed to be putting it all aside as he told Bolan, "Rudi is still the best of his kind, Omega. He never asks why or how. He only asks what."

"You're right," said Bolan-Omega. "They don't come like that in the new packages, do they?"

Folani did not mind being the subject of such praise. He stroked the auto, grinned at the lords of his realm, and went back inside.

"I meant it," said Copa, quietly. "Rudi's the best there is. And he's not so old. He's still mean as sin."

"Just don't give him much to think about," Bolan suggested.

"Oh, you're right there. I don't." The guy was loosening up. "But he's a perfect watchdog. The best. I say sit and he sits. I say hit and he hits. That's all I want from Rudi."

"That's all you need from Rudi," Bolan agreed. "Just keep him on the family jewels and you can rest your mind."

It was enough. Copa's gaze flicked to the barn as he responded to it. "You know about that, huh?" He chuckled, though without great humor. "You guys are the beatingest."

No, Bolan did not "know about that." But he was trying. "A bit here and a piece there, Nick," he explained while not explaining. "We haven't been nosing around. But we do hear things. You know?"

Yes, Nick knew. It was the Ace's duty to hear things. He said, "Right—you can't help that, I guess. Neither can I. Sometimes I—even—it's hard to keep a lid on, isn't it? The boys sometimes talk right out, in front of Mrs. Copa. I've told 'em and told 'em, and still they—what the hell can you do?"

"You keep her on a short leash, I guess," Bolan replied sympathetically.

"Right. That's all you can do. At least until I get it all safed. But—well I guess you noticed—it gets on her nerves. Hell, I hate that. But what can I do?"

The boss of Nashville was coming around, again. Not exactly jovial—but talkative, anyway. "You're doing it," Bolan assured him. "I wouldn't worry. She's a class lady. She'll pick up."

"Oh sure."

"You can't afford to risk a misstep, now."

"Hell no. I risk nothing."

Bolan could not nudge it beyond that. He, too, could not afford a misstep; he could not openly pry into the secrets of that barn.

Something else had become nudged loose during the exchange, though. The Mafia boss had relaxed somewhat and he seemed to be re-thinking his problem with Crazy Gordy Mazzarelli.

"You think I should try drawing Gordy out, eh?"

"Hey, Nick, forget it. I didn't come to tell you how to—"

"No, no, come off that. You're the troubleshooter. How would you handle it?"

Bolan sighed and took a couple more steps toward the barn. He very deliberately produced a cigarillo and lit it while shaded eyes probed the secrets of that interior. Then he turned back to Copa and told him, "I wouldn't walk straight up and hit him on the mouth, Nick. That could be a costly piece of satisfaction. I'd cool it, and watch him, and wait my chance."

That other voice was barely audible as it replied, "Do it, then."

Bolan shifted his gaze about fifteen degrees to the right as he asked just as quietly, "Did I hear your fingers snap, Nick?"

"You did."

They both knew the meaning of that. The troubleshooter had just received a license to hunt from the Lord of the Hills.

Bolan-Omega said, "You understand—once I start, there's no calling it back."

Copa sighed and said, "Just do what you have to do to save the investment. But do it quietly."

Bolan glanced at his watch as the distant sound of copter blades stole into the moment. Time was up. Grimaldi was nearby.

He casually put a hand into his coatpocket and punched the button on the microradio as he told his host, "My chopper is coming. It's time to go. But I'll be around. You'll give Gordy my message?"

Copa's lips twisted into a wry smile, but the eyes did not know it. "Cheese for the rat, huh?"

Bolan grinned soberly. "You said that; I didn't."

"Yeah but you've been working on me to say it ever since you got here. Don't deny it."

Bolan-Omega did not deny it. He said, "It's your territory, Nick."

"But it's your game," Copa said, still smiling wryly.

Bolan hoped that was true.

Yeah. He certainly hoped that it was.

## CHAPTER 12

# THE GAMESMEN

Grimaldi's eyes were looking a bit wild as Bolan climbed aboard and said, "Hit it."

They hit it, moving up and away before Bolan was fully settled into the seat. He put on the headset and told his pilot, "Perfect timing, Jack."

Grimaldi showed him a shaking hand and said, "I never get used to this."

"Neither do I," Bolan admitted.

"How'd it go?"

"Okay, I think. Do we have ground communications?"

"Yeah. I was just talking to them. Switch your headset over to the lefthand position."

"Got it. Can you hear me?"

"Right. Go ahead. You're on."

*"Rover, do you read Skyman?"*

Tommy Anders' delighted tones bounced

back through the earphone. *"Five by, guy. Do it."*

*"He bought it. Are you in position?"*

*"In place and waiting, old buddy. Is the game the same?"*

*"No changes at this time, Rover. But play it loose."*

*"I read the game the same and we play it loose. We gone, bye bye."*

Bolan switched the headset back to intercome and asked Grimaldi, "Did you hear it?"

"I heard it," the pilot tensely replied. "So now what?"

"So now we wait and watch and hope," Bolan told him.

"The story of life," Grimaldi replied, sighing.

Exactly. That was exactly what it was.


"He didn't stay long," Mazzarelli nervously observed.

"Not that guy," Copa said. "He's not here to fart around. Jeez, he's an impressive son of a bitch."

"What, uh, what's it all about, Nick?"

"Damned if I know yet. Makes no sense to me. You sure you told me all you know about that Leonetti kid?"

"God is my witness, Nick. So what'd the guy say?"

"About what?"

"About anything. Exactly what did he want?"

"Damned if I know for sure. Those guys

114

play it close to the chest. But he's going to be around awhile, Gordy. I want you to treat him right. That means stay out of his way."

"If that's what you want, sure."

"That's what I want."

"What's he looking for? What does Leonetti have to do with it?"

"I don't know for sure. He says Leonetti is Clemenza's man. But you know how these guys are. They don't say much. But I think he was sent by the sponsors."

"What made you think that?"

"Well, he's got a Full House."

"Yeh, but that comes from . . ." Mazzarelli nervously lit a cigarette. "I guess I don't understand how those—who sends those guys? I mean, how are they sent?"

"Hell, Gordy, *I* could send them."

"*You* could?"

"Sure. A year ago, no. Today, yeah. I just call the *headshed* and tell 'em I need someone. Whatever they send is whatever fits the problem. And whatever fits the sender. Now, see, I don't think I could draw a Full House, though. I mean, after all, let's be men, my horsepower isn't that high yet. Get me?"

"Okay, sure, I get that. You're saying a Full House means a lot of horsepower sent it."

"You got it."

"And you think he was sent by the sponsors?"

"That's what I think, yeah. Why? Does that make you nervous?"

Mazzarelli sent out a smoke signal from his

lungs as he replied, "A little, yeah. I don't like this kind of stuff behind my back. Neither should you."

"You want to call the sponsors and put in a complaint, Gordy?"

"I'm not saying that. I'm just saying I don't like it."

"Why not? If we're clean, what's to worry? Clemenza took a fall. Okay. That's not my fault. It isn't even my worry. I didn't set this thing up. And I'm not going to fall with it. But now of course if the sponsors think there's a way to pull it out, then sure, that's okay with me. I got money in this thing, too. If Omega can pull it out, who the hell cares who sent him?"

"Is that what he's here for?"

"What did I say?"

"You said to pull it out. How the hell can he pull it out?"

"I already said more than I meant to say," Copa growled. "Forget I said anything. You reading me, Gordy? Forget it."

"Okay, okay," Mazzarelli replied, backing off somewhat. "But I still think . . ."

"Who do you think, Gordy?"

"I think someone should keep an eye on that hotass. We all know what those guys tried to pull off under old man Marinello. I wouldn't trust them any farther than I can shoot, Nick. I mean that. Listen, something's funny in town already. Something's out of whack. While you were out jawing with that guy, I spent my time checking the action in town. Something's screwy. Certain people are suddenly nowhere. People are—"

"Certain people like who?"

"Certain people like Dolly Clark and Ray Oxley and Jess Higgins. Phones don't answer, or phones are busy or you get dumb answers. I don't like it. I think this guy is already taking a big walk through our territory, Nick. And I don't like it—no, I don't like it."

"You think you ought to be in town?"

"I sure do. I at least want to *know* what the guy is doing."

Copa turned away to be sure he didn't tip his hand with an irrepressible smile. He said, "Okay, Gordy. You go on in and safe your town. But you stay out of Omega's way."

The guy didn't even bother to thank him, or to acknowledge the okay—or even to say so long. He just got the hell out of there, moving fast, consumed by the need to protect his own little empire. And the boss of Nashville had to wonder as to the extent of the empire Crazy Gordy had already carved out for himself.

Yeah. The lord of any realm would necessarily wonder about such things. And he would move very quickly, too, to protect his own.

Copa gave Mazzarelli a couple of minutes to get clear before he punched the desk intercom to start his own move.

"Get the cars ready," he instructed. "We're going to town."

Damn right they were going to town.

Omega had been a hundred percent right.

117

And that fucking Mazzarelli was soon going to be 100 percent *dead*.

*"The quail is on the wing, Skyman."*

*"How many away?"*

*"We count two, coming out fast. Five to the flock."*

Which meant, Bolan thought, two vehicles each bearing five men. Mazzarelli with two full crews of headhunters, if the thing was working.

*"You've wired them?"*

*"They're wired."*

*"Look for more. And give me a quick hit when they show."*

*"Ten-four."*

Bolan explained to Grimaldi: "They'll all be flying before long. I hope. Hang loose, Jack. I may decide to call an audible."

The pilot replied, "Right. What'd you find in there?"

"I'm not sure. That's why the possible audible."

"Whatever that means," Grimaldi sighed.

"You still want a hard hand?"

"Whatever you need, Sarge. You know that."

Bolan gave him a sober wink. "Okay. Just remember you said it."

"Let it be my epitaph," Grimaldi replied. "No, I take that back. Let's not talk about epitaphs."

They were flying a holding pattern above the hills a few miles east of the Copa estate, well out of visual range of the little drama unfolding down below. A couple of minutes after the first contact report, another came: *"Ho ho and away we go! It's a convoy!"*

*"How many do you make, Rover?"*

*"They're still coming. I make . . . five . . . six . . . that's it, six and heavy."*

Lord Copa was coming out with a full house of his own.

Bolan replied to Anders, *"Okay, they're all yours. Play it close. I'll be working another angle."*

*"Is this a change in the game?"*

*"That is affirmative. You've got the quail. I'm taking the nest."*

Toby Ranger's voice swelled in with, *"Negative, negative, damnit! Let's play the call!"*

Bolan told her, *"You still have the percentage play, babe. Don't screw it up. I'm gone, bye bye."*

He turned off the radio and said to Grimaldi, "Okay, you're a hardman. Take us back."

"Back *where*?"

"Back *there*. Back to paydirt."

"You're out of your flipping mind," the pilot said—but already he was altering the pitch of the rotors, biting the atmosphere and lurching into an alignment toward the Copa hideaway.

Toward paydirt, yeah. Which was simply another way of saying *hellgrounds*.

Grimaldi's strained tones came through the intercom, "You sure this is what you want to do?"

What he *wanted* to do? Hell no, it was *not* what he *wanted* to do.

119

Bolan chuckled into the headset as he told his friend, the Mafia pilot, "I thought we were not going to talk about epitaphs, Jack."

"Who's talking about epitaphs? I'm talking about headstones," was the biting reply. "What's it all about?"

"We're going back, that's what it's all about. But I don't want anyone to know it. I want you to drop me into that joint clean, quick, and silent."

"That's impossible."

"So," Bolan replied with a sour smile, "that means you try a little harder. Right?"

"Wrong," said Grimaldi. "It means you die a lot quicker. But if that's what you want . . ."

It was not what Bolan wanted, no.

But it was what he had to do.

## CHAPTER 13

# TURNABOUT

A soldier who goes into combat with an over-riding desire to remain alive is not a good soldier. Bolan knew that. The good soldier is the committed soldier—one in whom the overriding desire is to achieve the objective, whatever the cost to himself.

And this was a war.

Toby Ranger knew it and Tom Anders knew it. Carl Lyons and Smiley Dublin had known it when they committed their own lives to the battle. They were all good soldiers.

So the SOG game in Nashville was not a rescue operation. The goal now was the same as in the beginning; nothing had changed except the circumstances. Bolan knew that Anders and Ranger were as concerned about the well-being of Carl Lyons as was Bolan himself. He also knew that this concern did not strongly affect the gameplan. They were still playing to win. Which is why they had called on Bolan instead of simply calling the game off and laying all over the opposition in a search and rescue mission.

They were good soldiers, yeah. And Bolan could respect them for that. He could also understand why Toby Ranger was so unhappy with him for calling an audible at the latest line of scrimmage. She had been concerned from the beginning that Bolan would play his own game instead of theirs—worried that he would blitz in and destroy an entire connective layer, destroying with it the SOG game of track and trap from street to penthouse.

Though they had been friends and even lovers, and though he knew that she respected his own private war, Bolan knew also that Toby had less faith in his approach than in her own. She regarded him as a local phenomenon, here today and gone tomorrow, a tragically temporary tool in the war on organized crime.

She had told him, once, during one of those rare Edenish moments, "I wish I could bottle you, Captain Courageous. That would be your greatest contribution. Maybe then we could inject a tiny squirt of you into every cop in the country. Not much—just one squirt per cop. Then we'd really see things happen in this clouted land."

He had replied to that in a playful tone. "Could we save a few squirts just for us?"

Her rebuttal, in typical Rangerese: "Don't be flip with me, hero. By the time you're done

122

with yourself, there'll be nothing left to squirt. You spend it with a fire hose nozzle, not with a hypodermic. When you're through gushing, we'll have to bury you with a syringe."

"Are we talking about love or war?" he'd asked her.

"Both," she told him. "You approach both like there's no tomorrow."

True. There was no tomorrow for Mack Bolan. He knew that. And it was why he did not like the quiet game, the waiting game. He had to do what he could while he could. And there was always just today.

But Toby could save her anxieties about *this* day. He was not here to kill their game. And he was not so fixated in his own brand of warfare that he could not play the quiet game for awhile. He was here to find Carl Lyons . . . dead or alive. He hoped to find him alive and well. And he would do all in his power to honor the SOG game. But when it came to the final cut—Lyons or the game—Bolan knew that he would come down on the side of Lyons. Because, really, Mack Bolan was not all that sold on the SOG game. He respected those people and he loved them one and all, but he did not believe that their answer to the Mafia was the best answer. He had seen too many such games played to futility—with all that grand investment of time and dollars and excellent manpower going down the drain while the crime masters of America went on strutting their stuff and thumbing their noses at the American justice system.

And, yeah, Bolan's answer was best. To those directly exposed to it, it was final. There were no legal maneuverings, no payoffs under the table, no judicial breastbeating for those who spat on the Bill of Rights. These guys knew the name of Mack Bolan's court. They knew also that they came in there naked and went out clothed in the final law of being. They went out dead—sentenced by their own deeds and executed by their own destinies.

*I am not their Judge.*

*I am their Judgment.*

*I am the Executioner.*

Bottle that, Toby. Then put it in an atomizer and spray it in the air that all Americans breathe, and then maybe all the SOGs everywhere could go home and play the quiet games of human love, and happiness, and fulfillment.

It would not happen, of course. One half of one percent of the American community would go on cannibalizing the rest of the body. And the gentle flocks would go on grazing, hardly taking note of the fact that their fellows were disappearing one by one, while harried shepherds patrolled the flanks with nets instead of clubs.

Bolan was no shepherd. He was a sheep, in wolf's clothing. And he carried the largest damned club he could find.

But okay, Toby—okay. He would keep the club sheathed for as long as possible, this time around. And he would play the SOG game—to a point. But that point was placed several paces to the life side of Carl Lyons' grave. This was no game of saviours and crosses. It was the game of life and death. For Mack Bolan, it was the only game in town.

"Would you mind telling me what is happening?" Grimaldi hissed through the intercom.

"In ten words or less?" Bolan asked lightly.

"In whatever it takes. This is as far as I go until—I need to know, if I'm going to—"

"You're right. Okay. As quick as possible, here's the lay. I believe that Mazzarelli's ambitions have exceeded his common sense. It looks like he's trying to pull off some cute game right under his boss's nose. I had only a small whiff of that before I went in there. But I followed the odor and I believe that I stumbled right into the thing. I still don't know what it is, for damn sure. But it seems a dead cinch that Leonetti figures in it somewhere. He—"

"Hold it. Leonetti?"

There were some things that Jack Grimaldi did not need to know, for various reasons. "Yeah, he's the key," Bolan explained, determined to skirt the truth a bit. "Does the name ring a bell for you?"

"Not really," said the pilot.

"Goes back quite a few years. Roberto Leonetti was a New York underboss whose ambitions exceeded his reach. A bit like Gordy, I'd guess. And he came to grief—had to go into hiding. His wife and kid were hustled away by one of his loyal soldiers who was caught and snuffed a few days later. The wife and kid were never seen again. Leonetti lived the rest of his days in hiding but he kept sending people out searching for the wife and kid until the day he died."

"They got to him, though?"

"They got to him, right. But not through the wife and kid. Like I said, they've never been seen since."

"So how does Leonetti figure—?"

"The kid came back."

"Oh. Uh-huh. So the kid *has* been seen. . . ."

"It seems that Dandy Jack Clemenza ran into him in Singapore while playing the heroin market. As the story goes, young Leonetti was heavily into the Golden Triangle loop. Guess it was in the blood—like father, like son. Clemenza took the kid on as his man in Asia."

"This kid is now grown up."

"Right."

"Great plot for a movie."

"It's no movie, Jack. A guy calling himself Carl Leonetti showed up here in Nashville last week. It seems that he's decided to go into competition against his own sponsor and—"

"That would be Clemenza."

"Right. It looks like Leonetti brought in a shipment that Clemenza knew nothing about. He was looking for a connection. He connected with Crazy Gordy."

"An unfortunate coincidence?"

"Depends on the point of view. It's a strongly layered outfit, Jack. Clemenza ran his own thing. Copa runs his own thing. Somewhere, several layers up, I'd guess, somebody runs both of them."

Grimaldi sighed. "And Mazzarelli just runs for Copa. Okay. Standard procedure."

"Sure. Standard split, too. The investment money comes down from the top and runs along the roots. As it's sucked back up, every wiseguy along the way skims off his share and sends the rest along."

"I understand that, yeah."

"Okay, understand this. The Syndicate got only half of what it paid for. That half fell the hard way last night in Memphis with Clemenza. The other half came into Nashville last week with Carl Leonetti."

"Oh ho," said the Mafia pilot in a falsely cheery voice. "I read that scene in big bold print."

"Read it this way, though. Leonetti hits Nashville with a shipment worth millions. He's trying to reach Copa. Instead, he reaches Mazzarelli. He's never seen again."

"Not even by Copa."

"Right. Especially not by Copa. So . . . I let it out. Now Copa is wondering about the name of the game."

Grimaldi chuckled. "So would I. But I still don't know what the hell—"

"I want Leonetti, Jack. I want him alive and well. The guy is wired."

"Oh. Oh. Yeah. Okay. That's why the feds."

"That's why, yeah."

"I couldn't figure it. It's not like you, Sarge."

"Maybe not, but that's the way it is. For now."

"So why are we going back?"

"You ever hear of Molly Franklin?"

"*The* Molly Franklin? Sure."

"She is Mrs. Copa."

"Awww—really? I never heard—"

"Neither did I. But he's introducing her that way. I take it that it hasn't been for long. She wants out, Jack. I'm going to take her out."

"Aw—well now—you mean we're . . . ?"

"Yeah. Mazzarelli is out chasing a Black Ace. Copa is out chasing Mazzarelli. I figure there couldn't be more than a handful of guys left at that joint. That's why I want you to slip me in there. There's a small stand of timber on the back forty. Did you notice it?"

Grimaldi sighed. "Yeah. I noticed it."

"If you pick your angle carefully, I believe you can come in behind that timber without attracting attention. A low profile approach. You know."

Grimaldi knew, sure. And he did not like it. "This just isn't like you, Sarge. If there's just a few guys there, why don't you just blast her out. I've seen you—"

"Not this time, Jack."

"That's where your odds are. Those trees are several hundred yards behind the house. It's open country from that point on. There's not even a bush between there and the house."

"I'll have to chance it," Bolan insisted.

"Let me fly over once more and—"

"No way. This is a soft mission, Jack. That lady has to simply disappear. I mean like into thin air."

"Well, I can get you closer than those trees."

Bolan had figured that all along. But it had to be the pilot's own choice.

"Without being seen?"

"I think so, yeah."

Bolan had confidence in the guy. With damn good reason. He took a long breath and said, "Okay. Do your stuff, flyman."

"You just watch my stuff," said Grimaldi.

Brave words, yeah. But the eyes were scared. Those knowing eyes were scared.

And, Bolan knew, with damn good reason.

## CHAPTER 14

# PROTOCOL

"They're going to hear us," Grimaldi warned Bolan. "There's no way to avoid that. So you'd better pray you've got your numbers right."

They were powering along just off the deck on a downwind approach, following the base of the ridge. Stunted trees growing along the 50-foot slope flashed past in dizzying procession just a few breathless centimeters removed from the reach of the windmilling blades.

And, yeah, Bolan knew that they would be heard. But he was counting on a greatly thinned human line in the defenses of that joint and he was especially counting on the fragility of human perceptions. Hearing was one thing; knowing, another.

The stone wall loomed up in the forward vision. The little bubbletop jumped it and powered on, hugging the ground again into the home stretch. Grimaldi had earned his combat stripes at 'Nam, and Bolan had confidence in the guy. He'd seen many such windmill jockeys perform amazing derring-do stunts in the combat zones. Grimaldi was as good as any in Bolan's experience. But he would never cease to marvel at the fantastic, precision control these guys could coax from the complicated flying machines.

They had scurried on for just a few seconds after hopping the wall when the pilot grunted, "Hang onto your socks!"

With no noticeable slowing of the forward speed, the little chopper suddenly wrenched upward. Bolan felt the G-forces where he sat and where he digested his food; the little craft shot skyward, rising abruptly like an elevator—straight up. Bolan caught a glimpse of the house at the top of the bounce, at about the same moment that he became aware that Grimaldi had killed the power. For a flashing instant it seemed that they were going to topple backwards, but then the little chopper righted itself and settled to the ground with hardly more impact than an ordinary landing. This one had been fast and quick—damned quick!

Grimaldi released his inner tensions with a happy whoop, then told his passenger, "Ground zero, buddy. Hit it."

But Bolan was already hitting it. The numbers were tight and there were none to be squandered on premature congratulations. The target was about 30 seconds away, up a 50-foot timbered slope and in through the aquatic gardens. Thanks to his daring jockey, Bolan figured he had a good chance. Yeah. Call it 50-50, anyway.

The whole place had been ominously quiet for more than ten minutes. And Molly Franklin knew that something very unusual was going on. Not that the place normally rang with joy, or anything like that. It had been so depressing an atmosphere around there for so long. . . .

But now it was just plain dead. Like a funeral parlor. The place had been buzzing, earlier. Really buzzing. When the bigshot from New York came in. All of the housemen were agog over his visit. Even old deadpan Lenny had begun nervously fussing over his "territory," lecturing the housemen in monosyllables about "protocol." That was really funny. Apes like those worrying about protocol. He *was* different, though. She'd sensed that difference even before he spoke. So maybe they were like that, at the upper level. But Nick would be at that level, some day. Maybe even Gordy. Somehow she could not imagine either of them there. They were nothing like . . .

She had stood at the window and watched as they strolled across the grounds. Watched and wondered. Was he telling Nick about her dumb plea for help? God, she felt like such a . . .

But he did seem . . .

Well maybe he was just being diplomatic. What did protocol mean? Family spat. Ha! Family *spat!*

133

The dirty bastard had taken her over. Some spat.

Had he really meant to make her think that he was going to intervene? And, if he had, was it diplomacy—protocol—or was it just . . . ?

Whatever, the place had become a funeral parlor very quickly. First, *he* left. Then Gordy and his funky legion. Then Nick and practically everybody on the place.

So what was going on?

Did it involve her?

She'd gone to her room and crammed the largest purse she could find with cosmetics and other dire necessities, then straight back to the garden. He *was* different. He was going to help. All this was some kind of protocol being worked on her behalf.

"You've got to pick your time and place," he'd said. "I always do that."

*So do it, beautiful. This is the time and this is the place. Everybody's gone. So where the hell are you?*

But she was just being dumb. Dumb, dumb, *dumb*! Nobody was going to help her! What the hell could anyone do, if Nick didn't want it done? Nothing! No, nothing!

She sat down beside the pool and drew her knees up to her chin, feeling desolate and alone.

Lenny came out and looked at her, started to say something but changed his mind, then sat down at a table and started toying with a dirty glass. Watching her. Someone was forever *watching* her!

She called to him, "What's going on, Lenny?"

"Just taking a breather, ma'am," he replied boredly. "Can I get you something?"

"You can get me the hell out of here!" she yelled.

The house boss just chuckled at that. He'd heard it often enough. She'd even tried seducing him, once. Hell, she'd do anything to get out. Anything. She'd kill. Damn right. She'd kill.

"You need a drink," he said to her.

"Go to hell!" she yelled at him.

He chuckled again.

Then she heard it. Lenny heard it, too. The helicopter was coming back. She lay on her back to get a better angle at the sky. Lenny got to his feet and took a couple of nervous steps toward the house.

He asked her, "Do you hear a chopper?"

She said, "I didn't hear anything."

"You'd better get inside."

"Go to hell, Lenny. I'll go inside when I want to go inside. Who're you expecting? The inspector-general?"

He ignored that and said, "Yeah, it's a chopper, all right."

She yelled, "Cheese it, Lenny, it's the cops! You'd better get your gun and hurry out there! They left you holding the bag, dummy! What're you gonna do now?"

He growled, "Please settle down, ma'am. This ain't no joke."

A man with a submachine gun jogged

135

around the corner of the glass-enclosed gardens. Lenny yelled at him. "Cover the pad, Jimmy!"

The man yelled back, "S'where I'm headed."

"You stay put!" Lenny snarled at her as he hurried into the house.

"You go straight to hell," she said, under her breath.

She stood up and hung the purse from her shoulder.

She was ready to go. Dumb, maybe, but she was ready for anything. Or so she thought. But she was not quite prepared for that which immediately happened. It startled her—scared hell out of her is what it did. She did not know where he came from or how he got there. But suddenly there he was, at her side, a hand on hers and that soft voice telling her, "Let's go. Quietly."

You bet.

Damn right.

And, scarey or not, she just loved his protocol.

# CHAPTER 15

# THE DEAL

As was so often the case, getting out was a bit more difficult than getting in. Time had a way of working for the other side in such situations. You can fool all the people anytime, sure—but not for very long at a time.

So Bolan was not all that surprised to find an obstacle in the path of withdrawal.

They were halfway down the slope and moving swiftly through the timber when Bolan abruptly came eyeball to eyeball with that obstacle. The guy was packing a grease gun close to the chest, and those eyes were both electrified and confused in the sudden confrontation.

Bolan's reaction was quicker and more positive. He doubled the guy over with a knee to the gut and snapped his neck in the spontaneous follow-through. The only sounds of the encounter were a grunting *whoof* from the midriff slam and the unmistakable pop of separating vertebrae.

The woman gasped with horror and fell to her knees in the underbrush.

Bolan set the safety on the grease gun and wordlessly handed it to the woman, then draped the dead man over his shoulder and continued the descent.

He heard her scrambling along close behind, breathing hard and beginning to come unglued. The grimness of her little adventure was settling in. He paused and turned back to tell her, "Come on. We're almost clear."

Those haunted eyes were now saucer-wide and inching toward hysteria—but she was fighting it. "I'm okay," she puffed. "Keep going."

Grimaldi was pacing the turf beside the helicopter with a revolver in hand. He wasted no time with greetings, but hopped aboard at first sight of them and fired the engine.

Bolan stowed his dead cargo behind the seat then lifted the lady aboard and moved quickly in behind her. The little craft leapt off immediately and resumed the ground-hugging flight along the base of the ridge. Seconds later they were around the bend, and lifting toward a more comfortable altitude.

Molly Franklin Copa, wedged small and shrinking between the two men, an automatic weapon on her lap, sat quietly with both hands covering her face.

Bolan donned his headset and told the pilot, "That was some kind of flying, Jack. Thanks."

138

"Say it again when I quit shaking," Grimaldi requested. "What's the cargo?"

"A Bad Luck Charlie," Bolan explained. "I couldn't leave it behind. Dead men *do* tell tales."

The pilot grunted an unintelligible response to that and turned a disturbed look toward the woman. "So do live women," he said with some discomfort.

"I think we'll enjoy her tales, Jack," Bolan replied. "Protect yourself, though."

"Yeah, sure." Grimaldi slipped on a pair of smoked glasses and donned a baseball-style cap. He grinned. "Think she'll give me an autograph?"

Bolan said, "I'm expecting much more than that." He plugged in another headset and placed it on Mrs. Copa's pretty head.

Yeah. A hell of a lot more than that.

So often, success is harder to live with than failure. Especially when success seems to come so easily. It had come to young Molly Franklin like a hand from heaven. She had "paid no dues," as the showbiz folk liked to put it. But it seemed that she'd been a good kid with warm ideals and a strong sense of gratitude— and that was the chief source of all her problems. She'd been a pushover for every sob story in town, an easy mark for sponging friends and relatives, and a sitting duck for all the vultures of the business who saw nothing but dollar signs when they looked at her.

So she'd had failure in success, agony with

her joys, frustration with triumphs. Ten years of that had set her up perfectly for Nick Copa. He caught her on the rebound from a second miserable marriage—at a time when her career was being threatened by a growing drinking problem and an incompetent business manager.

They were quietly married in Vegas following a whirlwind, sixty-hour courtship. And Copa immediately set about putting the Molly Franklin Company in order. Apparently he'd made a few offers which certain people could not refuse, because he cut through a stultifying legal process which could have taken years to accomplish. Almost overnight he fired her manager, switched her to a different booking outfit, killed an exclusive recording contract, and took over the whole works himself. Several days later he ran off all the loungers and spongers from Franklin Place, the ridge-top estate which had been Molly's home for several years, replacing them very quickly with his own cadre.

All of which had seemed highly commendable to Molly, in the beginning. She'd admired Nick's strength and hardnosed business attitude—and although she'd known from the beginning that he was mixed up somehow in the rackets, she'd loved and trusted him and welcomed his strong hand in her affairs.

She'd thought it a marvelous idea when he converted her barn into a recording studio, then began producing her records from there. She did not know until months later that the studio was also being used as a pirate factory for the theft of other people's recordings.

Ditto the television studio in the barn's loft. Except that they never got around to producing any Molly Franklin packages from there. It seemed that there was never any production time available between the endless one-reelers of hardcore porn being filmed and processed there.

"You saw a couple of the stars in the pool today," she told Bolan. "They live in. Like me. But they have a hell of a lot more freedom than I have."

Bolan said, "I saw some unopened crates in the barn. What's in them?"

"Must be the video cassette stuff," she replied.

"What's it for?"

"Oh that's the big, coming thing—casette players for television. It will probably make Nick a billionnaire. He wants to record TV shows and movies and sell them abroad—on the black market, of course."

Of course.

She went on: "But the thing I hated most . . ."

"Yeah?" Bolan prompted her.

"He's blackmailing people. And he's using me in that."

"Which people?"

"You know, official people. Politicians, mostly."

"How is he using you?"

"Oh I'm the bait—the celebrity, you know. I throw these big parties, see. And who in Nashville would turn down an invitation to a Molly Franklin party? And we have this live-in whore corps, you see."

Bolan growled, "I see, yeah."

"And these special bedrooms for special guests."

"Uh huh."

"Nick calls them the Candid Camera rooms."

"I get the picture," Bolan told her.

She sighed and said, "The victims never do. They pay and pay but they never get the pictures. They don't pay with money, of course. And these are moving pictures, and I *do* mean *moving*."

Things usually sound trite only because they are so true to form, so much a normal pattern. This one was trite as hell, the oldest trick in the bag—and that was because it worked so well. Obviously it had worked very well for Nick Copa in Tennessee. His entrenchment there had come with miraculous swiftness.

The lady was making that very point. "I guess Nick is about the most powerful man in these parts, right now."

"We'll see," Bolan told her.

"And he's built it all in less than six months."

"He could lose it a lot quicker."

"Does that worry you?"

Bolan-Omega shook his head. "Not a bit. Once a trench is dug, anyone can man it."

She got his meaning. "Okay. Doesn't worry me, either. I don't know why I've been telling you all this. You probably know all about it, anyway. Well listen . . . you never have to

142

worry about *me*. I'll never talk to anybody about this. I know better than that. But I do want you to get that man off my back."

He asked her, "What'd you have in mind?"

She shivered. "Whatever it takes. You can have the farm. I don't care if I never see it again. Make him an offer . . . I don't know. I don't *care*. Just keep him *away*."

Bolan said, "Okay. You have a deal. Can you believe that?"

She replied, "I guess I have to believe it, don't I. Okay. You want the man from Singapore. Right?"

So right.

And Bolan just had to believe that she could deliver. It was, after all, an offer which could not be refused.

## CHAPTER 16

# SQUARING IT

Toby Ranger answered the knock and stood at the doorway staring coldly at him for a moment before greeting him. "Well, look who's here. If it isn't Captain Cataclysm."

She turned her back on him and walked away.

Bolan pushed on inside, *sans* invitation, and closed the door.

Tom Anders sat behind a bottle of beer, near the window. Toby went into the bathroom, without looking back.

The atmosphere in there was decidedly chilly.

Bolan said, "I tried the radio and couldn't connect. This is the last place I expected to find you."

Anders growled, "You want a beer?"

Bolan waved the offer away. "Tell me about it."

Anders sighed and lit a cigarette. Following

145

a long silence, he replied, "There was a shootout."

"Where?"

"Inside the walls at the Juliana Academy."

Bolan took a cigarette also, and dropped into a chair near the door. "So. Gordy didn't streak for Carl, after all."

Anders said, "Not unless he expected to find him at the Academy."

"What *did* he find there?"

"A padlock and a legal notice on the door. He was very upset. Then Copa came roaring in as the Mazzarelli army was withdrawing."

Bolan sighed. "I was afraid of that."

"Yeah. Guess you stoked the fires a bit too warmly. But who can figure those guys? He came in shooting, Sarge."

"Who won?"

"Nobody won. Nobody lost. Talk about your gangs that can't shoot straight . . . those guys must have fired a zillion rounds. But they didn't leave much blood behind. Copa got his hair parted. Guess it was just a scratch. He was alive and raving last I saw him."

Bolan grunted and asked, "How about Gordy?"

"Yeah, how 'bout Gordy. We don't know. We lost 'im in the bustout."

"He split."

"Yeah, he split. Him and about half his army shot their way out. The other half slipped over the back wall and faded away. I guess. Broad daylight, too. I don't know how the hell . . ."

146

"You lost Mazzarelli."

"We lost 'im, yeah."

"How's Smiley?"

"Smiley will be okay," Anders replied feebly. "But she's no help in this. They kept her stupid for a week. She's lucid now but she knows nothing."

"The other people are still under wraps?"

"Oh sure. But they're giving nothing, either."

Bolan put out his cigarette and went to the window. He took a taste from Anders' bottle, made a face, said, "It's flat."

"That's not all that's flat," Anders replied, without emotion.

Bolan turned to look out the window. The voice was very soft as he inquired, "Why didn't you tell me that Nick was married to Molly Franklin?"

"It didn't seem pertinent."

"That's not for you to decide, Tom. When I ask for a briefing, I don't want you deciding what's pertinent and what is not. I expect a total package."

"Sorry. I guess none of us are perfect."

Bolan ignored the reflexive dig. "What else did you think was not pertinent?"

"What do you mean?"

He turned the icy blues straight onto his longtime friend. "You know what I mean," he said quietly.

Anders sighed heavily and broke the penetrating eye contact. "Yeah. I guess I do."

At that point, Toby came out of the

bathroom with a clatter. She struck a pose with hips outthrust and angrily said to Anders, "You tell him not a damn thing! You tell him nothing!"

Bolan growled, "Sit on it, Toby."

She said, "Go to hell! You blew it and you know you blew it. So don't come in here with your accusing eyes and bleeding hands and—and . . ."

Very quietly he told her, "I've located Carl."

That stunned her. Those great eyes flared as she gasped, "What?! Where?!"

Anders jumped to his feet, upsetting the beer. "Is he okay?"

Bolan turned a hard look his way. "You want a full briefing? Or do you want it SOG style?"

The little guy cried, "Jesus God, I—don't play with it, damnit! Is he okay or isn't he?"

Bolan very deliberately lit another cigarette.

Toby slumped to the floor and put her head on upraised knees. In a muffled voice, she said, "Okay, Captain Cute. We surrender. For God's sake. . . ."

"He's alive. And reasonably well. For the moment, anyway."

Anders gave not a sound. He turned quickly away and busied himself with the spilled beer.

Toby lay back on the floor and hiked her skirt up to the waist—then lay there spread-eagled with eyes closed, the lovely face composed and giving no hint of the rampaging emotions within. But the closed eyes were leaking fluid.

Bolan stood over her and took a long pull at the cigarette. He nudged a bare thigh with the side of his foot and growled, "Cut it out, Toby. What's this for?"

Her voice came small and contrite. "The symbolism should be obvious. You're right and I'm wrong. So ravish me. Both of you. Go ahead."

"You're lucky it's the wrong time and place, babe," he told her.

"Sarge, sit down." Anders said. "Let's square this up."

Toby opened her eyes and blinked back the moisture as she seconded the motion. "Please."

They were apologizing. He was accepting. "Okay. You first."

"Okay, so you're right," Anders said. "The dope traffic is a fringe issue. Nick Copa has been the mission goal all along. Anything beyond that is just pure haze, at the moment."

"Of course, the heroin was a very convenient point of entry," Toby said.

"So why all the cutesy?" Bolan asked. "Why didn't you just—?"

"Know where we're at? This could just be the home of our next president. It's politically sensitive territory," Anders said.

Toby: "But of course it's almost virgin territory for the Mob."

Bolan: "There no such thing as almost a virgin."

Anders: "Call it political virginity."

Toby: "It's still a virgin."

Anders: "The good old boys have just been

149

playing with them*selves* all these years. So that's technical virginity, anyway. But they've been ripe for rape for a long time."

Toby: "The rape became almost inevitable when a certain young senator suddenly began achieving such high national visibility. He's likely to be a presidential nominee the next time around."

Anders: "So the stakes are pretty high."

Bolan smiled soberly. "High enough to SOG it, eh."

Toby said quickly, "That's right. We weren't trying to con you, big man. But it *is* a highly sensitive operation. We were ordered to give it the full silk glove treatment."

"The double soft," Bolan murmured.

"Right," said Anders. "This Tennessee senator is a pretty straight guy. As clean as any. But he *is* a politician."

Bolan asked, "Does Copa have something on the guy?"

"Not yet. Bet your ass he's trying, though."

Toby said, "What he can't find he'll try to manufacture."

Anders: "We have the feeling that he's already clubbed a few others that way. But, see, this is all damned sensitive. I mean, if we came in here blowing whistles and waving a big stick—I mean, whether the guy is straight or not, he'll get dirtied. You know how things go in political life."

Toby: "It's the law of negatives. A single accusation is worth a thousand denials."

"And there's another law," Anders added.

"The law of reversal. If we don't do this cleanly, someone is bound to start yelling about dirty tricks."

Toby: "He means dirty campaign tricks."

Anders: "Right. We can't allow the *hint* of dirty tricks here. It could blow sky high. If this guy does get the nomination, he'll be running against the present administration. Our orders are to safe the area."

"Very quietly," Toby added.

Anders explained: "The present administration figures to be re-elected, anyway. They don't want—an emotional issue, even a false one, could swing the thing off center."

Bolan quietly asked no one in particular, "Are you people working for the White House?"

The soggers exchanged quick glances. Anders took it. He replied, "Ultimately, sure. He's the Commander in Chief, isn't he? But we serve the office, not the man."

Bolan sighed and said, "Where've I heard that before?"

"This is clean," Toby assured him.

Bolan said, "And your orders are to safe the area. What exactly does that mean?"

Anders: "Exactly what it says. We have to quietly neutralize all subversive political influences in the area."

"Subversive to whom?"

"Subversive to the national interest. We're not working for any election campaign, if that's what you're getting at. This operation is strictly on the level. It gets sensitive *only* if it gets political. We're supposed to keep that from happening."

"You're going to neutralize it."

"That's the idea."

"How?"

Anders sighed and shot a quick look at Toby as he replied, "Well, that is the problem, isn't it."

Toby said, "It's like toppling dominoes. If we could be sure that it is strictly a local problem—but it isn't pointing that way. And of course it is not just the politics. They—these people have a brand new playground here. And they can reach the entire world from right here. God, they're into just about everything."

Bolan said, "You better know it."

Toby told him, "We've been worried that you would take Copa out of play. Snuff him."

Anders hastened to add: "Too bad that it's not that simple. Copa is a nobody, in the national sense. We just don't know enough about the guy. Maybe he's no more than the local puppet. We cut his strings and where are we? Back to the beginning, that's where. And while we're scrambling around trying to pin the new puppet, we lose the game by default. So what's gained by a snuff?"

Toby said, "That's why Carl is so vital to the operation. We must get him inside, in a sensitive position."

Bolan softly inquired, "Via Singapore?"

"We were working another problem in that part of the world," Anders explained. "We literally fell into this Tennessee game."

152

Bolan said, "Stroke of luck."

"Exactly. Don't knock it. We take what we can get. A domestic outfit was already sniffing the Tennessee trail. It all came together at headquarters. So we take what we can get. Don't you?"

Bolan grinned. "Usually. I took Molly Franklin."

Toby asked, without emotion, "Dead or alive?"

He gave her a hard look. "Alive and kicking. She wanted out. I got her out."

"Wonderful. So you just called time, stopped the game, and got off to rescue a—"

Anders stopped her with a growl. "Toby! Don't start it up again!"

She replied, meekly, "Sorry."

Bolan said, "The Mob takes what they can get, too. I don't believe they came here looking for a political patsy. They came looking for the same old thing—a quick buck. Copa found his edge and moved it in. Virgin territory—yeah, maybe. But I don't see a grand conspiracy—no puppets, no puppeteers. It smells like a ground floor operation to me. The guy is trying to build something here. He has outside help, sure, but I think it's mainly in the form of financial support. Once it gets rolling—well, yeah, maybe so. Nashville could become the seat of the new empire. Right now there is no empire—none that counts. It has returned to the feudal system. Copa is no puppet. He's a lord, and this is his realm. He's the *man*. I believe if you took him out, right now, the whole thing would fall apart."

"Wow," Toby said softly, with mock surprise. "He walks *and* talks."

Anders growled, "Knock it off, Toby." He asked Bolan, "How strong is your feel on that?"

Bolan's gaze traveled from one to the other—then he clasped hands behind his head and stared at the ceiling. After a moment, he said, "I guess there's no reason to test it. We still have Carl."

"Where *is* Carl?"

"He's in a cabin out near Priest Reservoir."

"What's his circumstances?"

"He's a prisoner of war."

"Which war?"

"The one between Nick Copa and Gordy Mazzarelli."

"How long do you plan on leaving him there?"

Bolan sighed. His gaze came down and rested briefly on each of them as he replied. "I guess that's up to you."

Anders stared thoughtfully at his own hands for a moment. Toby started to say something then changed her mind.

Bolan said, "What?"

She said, "I guess it's up to Tommy."

Anders quietly said, "We'd rather not see Copa burn right away. Not until we *know* it's safed."

Yeah. Bolan could respect that. He asked, "Can Carl deliver on that heroin?"

154

"Sure. We have it safed away. He can have it with a phone call."

Toby said, "It's really very important. It's a side issue, like Tommy said, but it's also the key to the underground railroad. We can bust a hundred bigtime wholesalers with that shipment. And maybe we can bust a whole lot more than that."

"So you want Carl delivered to Nick Copa."

Anders said, "That's where we've been angling all along."

"So Lyons becomes Copa's horseman. Then what?"

"Then we begin the burn on Copa."

"How?"

"Carl will do that. Once he gets inside."

"How?"

Anders grinned as he replied, "Very carefully."

Bolan grinned back. "Yeah. He could do it, too."

"Sure he could do it."

Bolan said. "Okay. Before I forget—do me a favor. Tell Hal to get word to Sticker that the Full House turned the trick. Sticker is a worrier. He should be updated."

"Hal" was Harold Brognola, federal chief of everything. "Sticker" was the redoubtable Leo Turrin, inside man extraordinary, the feds' man at Mafia headquarters.

Anders said, "I don't know what it means but I'll send the message. A Full House?"

Bolan said, "Yeah. And it's getting fuller all

the time. I guess you'd better call in your fail-safe line, Tom. But give me operating room."

"What's the trick?"

"The trick is to safe an empire."

Toby sniffed and said, "I thought we were getting square."

"I've been there all the while," Bolan told her. "How about you?"

She dropped her eyes but then she flashed him a smile and replied, "*Touche*, Captain Quick. But don't you think *we* should be in the signals this time?"

Indeed, yes. Bolan the Quick would have it no other way.

"Just give me plenty of room," he said quietly.

## CHAPTER 17

# SAFING IT

Conditions were not exactly ideal for a night operation. There was a full moon, a cloudless sky, no wind anywhere. But it would have to do.

He was in blacksuit and soft footwear. The big silver .44 magnum rode the honor spot at the right hip. Close to the heart and snugged into a special shoulder harness was the whispering Beretta. Slit pockets at the outer calf of each leg carried surgical quality stilettoes. Nylon garrotes were coiled and waiting at the waist.

He had been scouting them for more than an hour. He had their numbers and he knew that Crazy Gordy was anything but crazy. The guy was a real pro. He knew how to set a defense. He had ten people on outside guard duty, as

157

silent as the night and well placed for maximum utilization of what was there.

Bolan had scouted the place earlier, during daylight, from a distance. And although he had spotted Carl Lyons strolling the grounds in the company of two keepers, there had been no other guards visible at that time. Now the place was crawling with them.

Which only made the job harder, not impossible.

But it would have been a hell of a lot simpler and surer if he had gone in while the boys were engaging themselves at Juliana Academy.

The cabin was emplaced on level ground in a relatively isolated setting. The Percy Priest Reservoir was a huge body of water, a major recreational area with a couple dozen parks hugging its shoreline. During daylight hours, the entire area had been busy with people. Not now. Now the whole world seemed deserted.

Except for that little cabin nestled in the trees.

There was activity in there, all right.

And silent sentries posted all around. Most of them carried sawed-off shotguns. They would be repeaters, bet on it. Two guys were hefting submachine guns. They were the anchor men—close in.

And there was a rover with nothing but a side-arm worn in a big shoulder holster. He was the most vulnerable. Therefore he would be the first to go.

The rover died without knowing it. A silent wraith in black stepped from behind a tree as the guy passed by. A razor-sharp stiletto expertly found its mark between the proper vertebrae of the neck and the rover dropped with a sigh.

Bolan quietly bore the body away and searched it. The only thing of interest was a small microradio clipped to the belt. The moonlight was so bright that he could read the *PocketCom* trademark on the little rig. It looked like a paging device, which it was—but it was also a two-channel CB radio.

A guy took what he could get, yeah.

Bolan took the tiny radio and returned to the hellgrounds. He quietly worked his way to within ten paces of the corner man at the left flank. The guy was wedged between the forks of a tree, about three feet off the ground, all but invisible. Bolan's thumb found the call button on the *PocketCom*. A rewarding beep responded from the tree—but the sentry did not stir. So Bolan did it again. This time he caught motion over there, followed by a hushed voice. "Who'd you want?"

The beep sounds for thee, guy.

Bolan had already started his move, taking quick advantage of the distraction.

And the left corner man never got his call.

Bolan left him where he died and went swiftly on. The radio was a godsend. All these guys were wearing them. The whole damn outfit was wired for sound, and Bolan held the sounder. Every guy in that yard beeped when Bolan pushed the button. And he had the entire left flank cleared out before the survivors began complaining.

"*Who's playing with the damn radios?*"

"*Henny! Has anybody seen Henny?*"

"*He passed here a couple minutes ago.*"

"*Get off the damn radios! Quiet it!*" Bolan recognized that harsh voice.

"*Someone's playing with the damn pager, Gordy. Or else somebody's in trouble.*"

"*Check it out, Henny. Give me a roger on that.*"

Bolan took the rear man with a singing garrote.

"*Henny! If you hear me, fire a shot!*"

The big silver AutoMag roared into the night and a flanker on the right forty yards uprange spun to eternity.

Another guy up there stepped from a shadow with a chopper poised, craning his neck for a better see. Big thunder erupted again, sending another 240 grains sizzling uprange to splatter that craning neck.

"*That's not Henny! Alla you boys—*"

The lights in the cabin went out.

People were in motion in the darkness.

Bolan was one of them, with them. He made the front porch and vaulted the railing, coming down softly on creaking boards. The body count had gone to seven. And he knew that the remaining three outside men had to be between the cabin and the access road.

And he had them coming in.

They were pulling back, cautious and trying to keep their dignity, moving slowly and passing quick signals back and forth in the interest of friendly identification.

All was entirely quiet inside the cabin. No voices, no movements. Which led Bolan to believe that not many were inside. Perhaps only two—one tied to a bed and the other. . . .

He waited for the outsiders to enter the cleared area at the front of the cabin. Three, yeah. One with a chopper. He took that one first, with a bone-shattering headshot that sent juices spraying into the moonbeams, then tracked immediately onto the other targets. Both shotguns boomed, almost precisely together, the loads traveling God knew where— certainly not toward the cabin—and not even the senders knew to where.

Ten up and ten down.

So how now, bad Gordy?

He fed a fresh clip into the AutoMag and kicked the door open. A revolver flashed at him from the dark interior and a heavy bullet whizzed past as he ducked back to cover.

He called in, "Come on out, Gordy."

"Who's there?"

"You haven't figured it out?"

A moment of silence, then, "I still hate your fucking town."

Bolan chuckled without humor. "Me too yours."

He flipped the spent clip from the AutoMag at the window. A shotgun boomed in there and the whole window dissolved.

A moment later: "You still there, Omega?"

"Oh sure."

161

"Why're you doing this?"

"You called me, guy."

"The hell I did. I'm just trying to make a living."

"You try too hard, Gordy. You should have known."

"Nothing ventured, nothing gained. Right?"

"Maybe so. You feel up to one more venture?"

The guy even *sounded* like Lou Costello as he asked, "Do I got a choice?"

"Guess not. I came for your head, Gordy."

"Hell you think I didn't know that right from the start? Well okay. You'll have to come and get it, hotass."

"Is that your final word?"

"It sure is."

The guy had not changed position during that conversation. Bolan had a pretty decent fix on the location of his voice. He just hoped to God there was only one.

He tried for a final fix. "Nick said I should kiss you first. I told him you're too damned ugly."

"Nick is a—"

Bolan would never know Crazy Gordy's final thoughts on Nick Copa. He'd launched himself with the first syllable of the reply, diving in through the shattered window with a twisting plunge to land bellyup.

The shotgun *baloomed* almost in the muzzle of the thundering .44, the flash lighting that interior like the single pulse of a strobe, Gordy's contorted face frozen there in a mask

162

of death as a heavy bullet blasted through clenched teeth and exploding flesh.

Bolan lay panting, knowing that he also had taken some heat, loathe to explore the extent of the damage.

But then a weak voice from the rear came like a candle in the gloom. "That you, Sarge?"

"Yeah."

"You okay?"

"Yeah. You?"

"Oh they've been treating me pretty well here. Exercises in the yard twice a day and—where's Smiley?"

"She's okay, Carl."

"Thank God. Well are you going to lay there and breathe or are you going to get me out of this mess?"

"I'm going to lay here and breathe. How about you?"

"I got no choice."

"Uh huh."

"I'm tied up, damnit."

"Do tell." Yeah, he'd taken some heat. The blacksuit was shredded at the left thigh. And there was some raw meat down there. Nothing big. But another silly millimeter to center and . . .

He got to his feet and tried it.

"Sure you're okay?" Lyons asked in that enfeebled voice.

"Guess I'm as good as you," Bolan replied, sighing. "You ready to go?"

"Hell yes I'm ready to go. But I'm not walking so well, Sarge."

163

"Think you've earned a ride?"

"For what? Rest camp? It's been a breeze."

Bolan doubted that. Gordy's plans were too ambitious to risk killing his golden goose before he got what he wanted from him. But there were lots of ways to hurt a man without killing him.

He snapped on the penlight. Mazzarelli was a mess. So was the cabin. A one-room affair— kitchen, bedroom, all in one.

Lyons was lashed to an old iron bedstead, hand and foot.

Bolan found the light switch and turned it on.

The poor guy was black and blue all over. And there were fresh hurts over old agonies. But he was all there. Thank God, all of him was there.

## CHAPTER 18

# SEALING IT

Grimaldi elevated a thumb and said, "This is getting like an unhealthy habit. Watch yourself."

Bolan released the seat belt as he told his pilot, "You can relax this time, Jack. It's all our way, now."

"I'll believe that," Grimaldi growled, "when I'm seeing this joint for the last time."

"Soon," Bolan promised, smiling grimly.

He stepped onto the pad at Franklin Place, paused halfway to the house to put down his package and light a cigarillo, and waited for the reception committee.

He sensed people all around him though he could see none. All the lights were on, inside and out. The grounds were lit up like a shopping center parking lot.

But apparently there was to be no formal reception.

He picked up his parcel and went on. The house boss met him just outside the door. Bolan said, "How's it swinging, Lenny?"

The guy was in a pout. He replied, "Just barely, sir. Mr. Copa ain't feeling so well, either. He wants you should get comfortable in the garden. He'll be with you in just a second. Uh, pardon me, sir. What's in the sack?"

"It's for your boss, Lenny."

"Oh, right—right, sir. Uh, can you find your own way? I'm a little short-handed."

Like hell he was.

But Bolan found his own way to paradise. And this time there were no prop cuties in the pool. No white-jacketed housemen were on hand to fuss over his comfort, either. The whole place was ominously quiet.

He placed the paper bag on the floor of the patio. Then he dragged a chair to poolside and straddled it, arms on the backrest, the cigarillo clamped between his teeth—in plain view from everywhere.

Someone turned on the underwater lights in the pool.

He chuckled and flipped the cigarillo into the illuminated water.

Copa came out a moment later. A large bandage completely covered the crown of his head. He'd lost some hair there, yeah. The face was pained, sour.

"I took a hit," he explained.

The guy was just standing there, about ten paces out, almost on top of the sack.

Bolan said, "I heard. I'd say you took a lucky one. Hurt much?"

"That's what the doc said. And, yes, it hurts like hell."

"All wounds heal quick in paradise, Nick."

"Don't talk to me about paradise," Copa growled. "Right now I got twenty evil demons kicking inside my head."

Bolan gave a philosophical shrug. No sympathy. "You'll get over it. And it'll make a nice chapter for your autobiography."

The guy scowled and asked, "Is that supposed to be some kind of dig?"

"No. I meant it. You should write that book some day. Change the names, of course."

"Of course."

The Lord of Nashville lit a cigar.

"Lenny tells me you brought something with you. What's in the sack?"

Mack Bolan had always been a man who could command himself. But what was in that sack had taken the strongest command he could muster. "Special gift," he said coldly. "A token of my esteem."

Copa bent cautiously over the paper bag and delicately opened it. He stared at the contents for a long moment then straightened up with a twisted smile.

"I like your style, Omega," he said quietly.

Sure. Bolan had known that he would. And if a guy wanted in the game then he had to be

167

prepared to participate in the rituals. *All* of the rituals. Still . . .

He reminded his host, "You snapped your fingers."

"Damn right I did," Copa gloated.

He gave the sack a vicious kick.

Crazy Gordy's bloodied head fell out of it on the first bounce and rolled into the pool. A new decorative touch to paradise.

Bolan lit another cigarillo.

Copa paced around for a moment, glaring at the thing in the pool, then he pulled up a chair close to the bearer of gifts and sat down.

"How many times you been here today?" he asked coldly.

Bolan replied evenly, "This is the third trip."

The guy chewed his cigar for a moment. "Uh huh. It figures. Never mind how you did it. Just tell me *why* you did it."

Bolan smiled soberly. "Call it an inspired act."

"What inspired it?"

"She did. Said she wanted to help. I believed her."

Copa snarled, "I want her back here! You hear me? I want her *back*!"

"The honeymoon is over, Nick. The lady doesn't want to come back."

"I want to hear her say it!"

Bolan shook his head. "Too late. We made a deal."

"What d'ya mean, we made a deal! Our deal was—"

"Not you and me, Nick. Me and her. She wanted out. So I took her out."

"That's the most outrageous damned—" The guy turned very pale. "Wait a minute! You didn't! . . ."

Bolan moved the idea away. "Hey, she's okay. I just did you both a favor. She'd become a liability to you. Much longer and she'd have become a *dead* liability. You get my meaning."

Copa got the meaning. "You did me a big favor, eh?"

"It's your only loss. Out of it all, Nick, your only loss. Count the possibilities. You could have lost it all."

A moment later, "How?"

Bolan spread his hands. "Why am I here?"

"You're here because I let you in."

"Wrong."

"Wrong?"

Bolan pulled a playing card from his breast pocket and snapped it toward the lord of Nashville. It sailed through the air and dropped at Copa's feet. And it did not matter which side came up; the ace of spades adorned both sides.

Copa placed a foot on the card and asked, "Is that for me?"

"It could have been."

"Why?"

"It didn't look good, Nick. They were wondering."

"About *me*?"

"Trade places. Wouldn't you wonder?"

The guy showed him a pasty smile as he replied, "I guess so. But they know better, now."

169

"They will, yeah. Soon as I get the report back."

"Well don't waste too much time doing that."

Bolan smiled coldly. "Just so we understand it, Nick. The report *does* have to get back."

Copa laughed over a private joke. Then he sobered abruptly to ask, "What's all this have to do with my wife?"

"Nothing," Bolan told him.

"Nothing?"

"Except from me to you."

"I don't get it."

Bolan got to his feet, nudged the paper sack into the pool with his foot, and returned to his chair. "It's clean now. Leave well enough alone. The lady helped me. I helped her back. Call it quits at that. Leave her go, Nick. That's from me to you."

Lord Copa pulled his chair closer. He was mad as hell. But he was trying to cool it. Presently he said, "Okay. I guess I can live with that. You better hope you can, too. I guess you know what you're doing. For me, it's a small enough loss."

"That's the way I saw it."

"Yeh."

"Did I hear you say thanks?"

"You heard it. So. Now, what about the Leonetti punk?"

Bolan said, "Just the way we figured it. Gordy was going for the whole pie. He snatched the kid and took him to a cabin out near the reservoir."

"I never heard of it."

"Gordy was the kind to keep secret places. Even from his boss. Especially from his boss."

Copa growled, "Crazy Gordy was a fink."

"More than that. He was a thief who stole from his own father and brothers."

Copa said, "He was a rotten shit." He spat at the pool.

"It was a one shot deal. He never planned to work with Leonetti. He just wanted to rob him. That means robbing you. And your friends. He put the kid on ice while he checked him out. Meanwhile he was working the kid for all he could get."

"How much was that?"

Bolan smiled soberly. "Not a damn thing."

"That's nice. That's damn nice."

"The kid checks out clean. He's got the stuff. It was to be Mazzarelli and Clemenza, not Mazzarelli and Leonetti. But the kid blundered in and spoiled their game. He didn't like the smell of the deal. That's why he came. He was trying to get to you when Gordy snatched him away."

Copa smiled craftily and said, "You knew he was clean all along. When you first came in here, you knew it. That's why you were cat and mousing me and Gordy. You wanted to see which one would take the break."

Bolan smiled at the Lord. "You're a big man, Nick. I'm glad it worked out this way."

The Lord was smiling back at the Executioner. "Me too," he said grandly. "You're not so small, yourself. Well. Well this is just wonderful. It calls for a celebration. We'll have some—"

Bolan held up a hand and said, "No offense, but I can't stay." He stood up. "Leonetti's at the Holiday Inn. A bit worse for a week of wear with Crazy Gordy but I think he'd probably enjoy a celebration, himself, right now. He's waiting for your call. The kid held out for a whole week, Nick. Now you and I both know what kind of guts that takes."

Lord Nick knew, sure. His eyes were shining as he said, "I've been looking for a kid with real guts for a long time, Omega. A man has to think of the future. Right?"

Omega replied, "Oh right, right."

"What's the kid's first name?"

"His name is Carlo. They call him Carl."

"Carl and me will get along just fine."

The Black Ace was sure of that.

Yes. He was very sure of that. For as long as Nick Copa's future might last.

Which, after all, was saying not a hell of a lot.

# EPILOG

Bolan checked in the rented car and stepped outside to the darkness of the service apron to await his pilot. He walked straight into Toby Ranger.

She said, "Leaving without saying goodbye, Captain Chicken?"

"Did you come all the way out here just to say it?"

She wrapped an arm inside his as she replied, "No. I thought I'd give you one last chance."

"At what?"

"At me. You don't really have anywhere to go tonight, do you?"

His regret was genuine. "I'm afraid so. Maybe there will be another time, Toby."

"Probably not," she replied spiritedly. "Well okay. Don't say I never offered. Uh, the others send their love. Carl got his call. He'll be meeting with Copa at midnight."

"Good. That's good."

"You're quite a guy. Know that?"

"Thanks. You're quite a gal."

"All's forgiven, then?"

"What's to forgive? We did the job, didn't we?"

She said, "I mean—well, you know. My mouth doesn't always have it together. And I go a little crazy sometimes. It's the damn work, I guess."

Yes. Bolan guessed that was true.

"And to tell the pure truth, Mack—I guess I couldn't get Georgette off my mind. That crazy night in Detroit. You know."

Sure. Bolan knew.

"I was afraid you were going to find Carl or Smiley like—like you found Georgette. I knew you'd go crazy if you did."

Maybe so, yeah.

"And that's why I was so uptight. You know I love you. And you know that I worry about you."

No, he had not known that.

He said, "Toby—"

"No, don't say anything. Nothing obligatory. I just wanted to . . . apologize."

Bolan grinned. "Must have been damned hard."

She smiled back. "Damned right."

He took her in his arms and kissed her; slowly, thoroughly; it was a very warm embrace. Certainly he knew where all of her was

174

at. And he told her, "There'll be other times, Toby."

"I know there will," she whispered. "Take care of all that beauty, huh?"

He said, "You too."

She faded quickly, then, like so many of Mack Bolan's dreams.

He was still looking at the spot where she'd stood when a heavy voice from the wall of the building declared, "She nearly nailed you that time, Striker. It was getting downright embarrassing."

The man who stepped from the shadows looked more like a Wall Street executive than what he really was: the ranking cop in the country, the one and only Harold Brognola, chief of the U.S. government's official war against crime.

Bolan shook a warm hand as he said, "Fancy finding you here. You're a bit late. It's all over."

Brognola grinned with the reply: "I've been here longer than you. Which says something for your methods, I guess."

"I got lucky."

"Baloney. Luck is something we make for ourselves. You make it all, guy. We thank you."

Bolan said, "You didn't go to all this trouble just to tell me that."

"Course not. I thought I'd offer you an overview."

"Of what?"

"You know how it is when you're wandering

through a forest? How all the trees look alike. I thought I'd give you a late picture of the forest."

"Okay."

"We don't think you've seen it lately."

"Seen what?"

"The forest. It's looking cleaner now than at any time in recent history. Thanks to you, mostly. The whole thing is coming unglued, Striker. Ever since New York. That really hurt them. They've lost faith in themselves. And there goes the quote organization unquote. They're scared, disoriented, afraid to trust anybody. And not a soul in Wonderland is reluctant to give you full credit for all that."

Bolan said, "Okay. Thanks for the vote. And thanks for the overview. But let's get to the bottom line. What are you really telling me?"

"We think maybe you broke their backs completely here in Tennessee. Or, that is, you've provided us with the tools to break them finally, forever."

"I can't buy that, Hal. These guys are a long way from finished."

"Sure. That's true. But it's coming apart under them. This is the overview we're trying to give you. Let me put it in your own language: we've just landed at Omaha Beach. The rest is preordained."

Bolan chuckled as he told the fed, "You wouldn't be forgetting the Battle of the Bulge or any of that good stuff."

"Like I said, though, it's preordained. The rest is pure mop-up."

"I hope you're right," Bolan said. "So where is that bottom line?"

"We have a consensus that—you shouldn't be wasting—you're too effective a soldier to be wasting your talents on a mop-up. Other people can do that, just as well. Maybe better. There's larger work waiting for you."

"Where?"

"Just look around. The Mob isn't the only devil loose in the land."

"Bottom line, Hal."

The chief fed sighed. "Hear it out. Don't jump at me. I've, uh, again been authorized to make you an offer. It includes full, official forgiveness and total remission of sins. And a free hand."

"How free?"

"As free as it can get under our form of government. You'll report directly to the National Security Council. You will—"

"That's no good, Hal. Sorry."

"I asked you to hear me out, damnit. *I* report to the NSC, you know. What that means, bottom line, is that I report to the President. Okay. Unruffle a bit. What it boils down to is a new chair at NSC. That new chair is your chair if you want it."

"I'd make a lousy bureaucrat."

"So do I. So what? I don't play their damn games, do I?"

Bolan chuckled. "What's the name of that chair?"

Brognola hesitated a moment for a bit of

dramatic play, then replied *sotto voce,* "Sensitive Operations."

It was Bolan's turn to hesitate, but not from any dramatic considerations. He said, "SOG Chief, eh?"

"You've got it. But it's a brand new chair with its own authority. Equal to mine. What d'you say?"

"I say it sounds interesting. If everything you've said is true."

"I wouldn't shit you, guy."

No, Bolan did not believe that he would. He said, "Let me think it some."

"You would undergo an entire alteration of identity. But that should be a snap for you. And we've got the most bewildering damned problems facing us. We need—you're the man—I don't know anyone else could fill the job. And think of the positives. It would get what's left of the Mob off your ass. Not to mention a million or so cops."

"What kind of problems?"

"Huh?"

"You said bewildering problems."

"Oh, hell. Pick them from the hat. International terrorism, for one. Political intrigues in emerging nations—there's one that can spread to infinity. Sensitive military operations. Special diplomatic missions. You'd get the full territory."

"I couldn't sit at a desk, Hal."

"You won't *have* a desk, buddy."

"I'd have to pick my own key people."

"Naturally."

"You think the Mob is about finished, eh?"

Brognola squeezed his neck as he replied, "More or less, yeah. We'd expect you to, uh, keep on top of any resurrections in that area, of course. And, look, you're going to find echoes of the Mob in everything you touch. It's the same war, guy, the same kind of enemy. You haven't been fighting *people*, you know. You've been fighting a *condition*."

Yeah, Bolan knew that. He said, "Let me think it, Hal."

The fed shoved a thin briefcase at him. "The particulars are in here. After you've read it, burn it. Then sift the ashes and burn it again. Let me have your decision within twenty-four hours."

Bolan accepted the briefcase, gave the guy a solemn smile, then turned away and walked toward the waiting plane.

SOG Chief, eh?

A new identity. A new life. Maybe even a new hope. Like a reprieve and a restart.

And end to the bloody last mile?

It was, yeah, a hell of an interesting offer. And he would think it some. Very carefully.

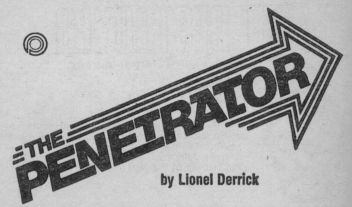

# THE PENETRATOR

### by Lionel Derrick

Mark Hardin. Discharged from the army, after service in Vietnam. His military career was over. But *his* war was just beginning. His reason for living and reason for dying become the same—to stamp out crime and corruption wherever he finds it. He is deadly; he is unpredictable; and he is dedicated. He is The Penetrator!

Read all of him in:

| Order | | Title | Book No. | Price |
|---|---|---|---|---|
| _____ | # 1 | THE TARGET IS H | P236 | $ .95 |
| _____ | # 2 | BLOOD ON THE STRIP | P237 | $ .95 |
| _____ | # 3 | CAPITOL HELL | P318 | $ .95 |
| _____ | # 4 | HIJACKING MANHATTAN | P338 | $ .95 |
| _____ | # 5 | MARDI GRAS MASSACRE | P378 | $ .95 |
| _____ | # 6 | TOKYO PURPLE | P434 | $1.25 |
| _____ | # 7 | BAJA BANDIDOS | P502 | $1.25 |
| _____ | # 8 | THE NORTHWEST CONTRACT | P540 | $1.25 |
| _____ | # 9 | DODGE CITY BOMBERS | P627 | $1.25 |
| _____ | #10 | THE HELLBOMB FLIGHT | P690 | $1.25 |

**TO ORDER**

Please check the space next to the book/s you want, send this order form together with your check or money order, include the price of the book/s and 25¢ for handling and mailing, to:
PINNACLE BOOKS, INC. / P.O. Box 4347
Grand Central Station / New York, N. Y. 10017

☐ Check here if you want a free catalog.

I have enclosed $_____check_____or money order_____as payment in full. No C.O.D.'s.

Name_____

Address_____

City_____State_____Zip_____
(Please allow time for delivery)

PB-4